D0883945

The Psychologist

The patient, who had been tilting her head up to look at me from beneath her wet hair, moved with sudden speed, pulling herself from Nurse Heather's grasp. She grabbed my arm and yanked us both to our knees. I found myself gazing into a single golden-brown eye, bright as it gave me a gimlet stare. The rest of her face was obscured by her hair.

Before I could pull myself from her, she shook her head, violent and distressed. "You must help her. You're the only one who can."

Startled and stunned, I froze where the patient held me. "Help who?" It was the only thing I could think to say. I tried to get a better look at the woman's face, but she shook her head again, hair still hiding her face. One bright golden eye—lucid despite the drugs in her system—stared back at me.

"It's within her. It was too much for me. Too many things to care for. I couldn't…She needed it…I didn't know what she'd do… the protection failed. You have to help her."

I put my hand on hers, keeping my voice calm. "I do not understand. Whom do I need to help?"

The grip on my arm tightened even as the lucidity in that single eye dimmed and dulled. "Don't make me rip the scales from your eyes. Don't make me. It'll change you forever. It'll change me, too. Please, don't make me do it!"

Cover illustration by Shane Pierce.

Color insert artwork by Jeff Lee Johnson and Tiffany Turrill.

ISBN: 978-1-6334-4319-8

Printed in the United States of America.

Fantasy Flight Games
1995 West County Road B2
Roseville, MN 55113
USA

Find out more about Fantasy Flight Games
and our many exciting worlds at

www.FantasyFlightGames.com

An

ARKHAM HORROR™

Novella

To Fight the Black Wind
by Jennifer Brozek

Fantasy Flight Games

Welcome to Arkham

IT IS THE HEIGHT OF THE ROARING TWENTIES. Flappers and young fellas dance the Charleston at raucous jazz clubs gleaming bright with electric lights. Beneath this gilded glamour, bloody turf wars rage, funded by gangsters and crooked cops who frequent rival speakeasies and gambling dens.

Amid these changing times, old New England towns hold their secrets close. Off the Aylesbury pike, in reclusive Dunwich, rolling hills hide decrepit farms and witch-haunted hollows. Past Cape Ann, the remote fishing village of Innsmouth rots from within. At the mouth of the Miskatonic River, mist-shrouded Kingsport lies dreaming. All the while, historic Arkham broods on the upper banks of the Miskatonic, its famed university delving into the world's darkest, most ancient mysteries.

Arkham's citizens insist everything is normal in their sleepy town, but horrific and bizarre events occur with increasing frequency. Strange lights flicker and people disappear in the forest beyond Hangman's Brook. Misshapen silhouettes prowl graveyards and shorelines, leaving savaged corpses in their wake. Nightmarish artifacts and disturbing tomes have surfaced, chronicling gods and incantations the world has tried to forget. Cavalier scientists have glimpsed far-flung worlds beyond our own that shatter the known laws of reality. Are these events somehow connected? If so, what calamity do they portend?

Those who dare investigate these incidents witness the inexplicable. Having seen such phenomena, they can never regain their old view of the world. Now that they know the hideous truth, they cannot run or hide from it. Just beneath the reassuring veneer of reality—a veneer that was never meant to be worn away—are forces that can drive the average person to despair. Yet, a rare few try to avert the end of the world, knowing it may well cost them their lives or sanity.

These investigators must rely on their wits and skills to learn as much as they can before it's too late. Some may find courage in the grace of a rosary, while others may burn away their fears with a swig of bootleg whiskey. They must try their hand at unpredictable spells that could doom them, or take up rifles and revolvers to combat foul creatures plaguing the night. Will it be enough?

Chapter 1

There are events and people that change your life forevermore. It is rare, though, that we acknowledge these occurrences. My perspective, my worldview, my life has been so altered I feel I must record what happened. I will always remember this week as a turning point. I will always remember Josephine as the catalyst for that change.

It began as all such things begin—on an ordinary day. I had seen all of my regular patients. Then I met my newest patient, Miss Josephine Ruggles. Our first meeting was a study in power dynamics between patients and doctors.

Josephine, heiress to the Ruggles Publishing fortune, sat on the edge of an overstuffed chair, her back straight and chin raised. She had not yet become one of the anonymous unfortunates of the asylum, shuffling to and fro with slumped shoulders and vacant eyes. She still wore a fine linen dress of pale yellow that enhanced her warm, tawny-beige skin. Her ebon hair still held organized curls gathered in a bow. A small gold cross adorned her neck.

At first glance, Josephine was a lovely young woman of good manners and quality breeding. That is, if you ignored the pale blue dressing gown she wore over her linen dress. Ignored the darkness under hollow brown eyes and did not see the slight tremble to hands *that clutched at the heavy silken fabric of a robe not usually worn out of the bedroom.*

Her malady—nightmares that left her bloody—seemed, at first, to be a common self-harm complex. Then I looked at the wounds. The mind is powerful, but I have never seen the mind create wounds like these.

Little did I know her wounds were just the first of many mysteries I would face while caring for Josephine.

"You do not believe me, Dr. Fern." Josephine's voice was a smooth contralto, roughened by fatigue.

It was a challenge designed to bring about a black and white reaction—disbelief brought distrust while belief allowed the patient to manipulate the doctor. I did neither. "We have yet to begin our first session, Miss Ruggles." As Josephine pondered this, I noted which drugs my new patient was taking. All were designed to give blissful, dreamless sleep.

Josephine gestured to the notes in my hands. "You began when you read those, *Doctor*. You do not believe me."

What would I not believe? My patient had nightmares, despite the medication she took to prevent such things, and she harmed herself at night. Something in the way she said "Doctor" made me wonder what kind of encounters she had had with Dr. Mintz. Perhaps that was where her aggressive stance stemmed from.

There was nothing specific in her records. Then again, many of his more esoteric experiments were never written about in public files. I kept the distaste from my face as I took a seat in the chair next to Josephine's. "I am listening. Please, tell me what you think I do not believe."

Josephine sighed. "The wounds—the *words* on my back. You do not believe they were caused by things in my dreams. Even when they are in places I cannot reach. Even when they are fresh and lined as if made by a printing press."

None of what Josephine was suggesting was possible, of course. However, in the beginning, I always allow my patients a way out of their fantasies. A way to prove or disprove their statements. "I have not seen your wounds. I cannot judge them."

Josephine stood as if jerked by marionette strings. She turned her back to me and opened her robe. With the almost soundless crumpling of fabric to the floor, the reason for the robe became clear: The back of the linen dress was stained red-brown. The rows of weeping wounds pressed their image into the cloth. It was even and regular. While it was unusual for patients to be so careful with their self-inflicted wounds, it was possible.

"Malachi. He told me once that you might understand. That you had tried to help him."

I twitched from my examination of Josephine's back and the hieroglyphic bloodstains in linen.

"Malachi?" How could she possibly know the name of my murdered patient from Providence Sanatorium? There was no earthly way she could know of him, an itinerant man in another part of the state.

"Yes, Malachi. I used to see him in my dreams. He is gone now. I have not seen him in a long time." The beautiful woman turned in one controlled, smooth motion—another testament to her inner strength and spirit, yet unbroken by the asylum. "Do you understand? Do you believe me?"

I did not. She spoke to Malachi in her dreams? How was that possible? It was not, of course. Josephine could not be speaking of my murdered patient. That would be ludicrous. She had to be speaking of another Malachi. After all, she was speaking of conversations in dreams.

I covered my confusion by taking Josephine's robe and standing. I offered it to her with a gentle smile that the hid the turmoil within. "Perhaps we should begin at the beginning. Pretend I know nothing. We will go from there."

Josephine stared at me for a long, timeless moment before she accepted her robe and slid it on. She nodded once. "The beginning then. Such as it is."

The pounding of my heart was loud in my ears as I took my seat once more. I tried to put the very idea of Malachi out of my mind. My patient was before me. She needed my help. If I listened close enough, I would understand her true trauma. I focused the whole of my being upon her.

Five heartbeats later, Josephine joined me, once more the unruffled young woman of high society. Despite her calm demeanor, the mask of her control was cracking: the unconscious flicks of her eyes about my office lingered on the windows and door as if seeking escape. If I did not work quickly, I would lose her to the asylum.

"The beginning. Three weeks ago, I woke up screaming. Even as my maid rushed into my chambers, the nightmare faded. All I remember now is a spiral of symbols and a labyrinth of woods." Josephine paused, glancing at me.

I nodded encouragement, my pen and my voice silent. It was standard fare so far. Images of being lost or out of control. I wondered what had happened three weeks ago to bring this about. I would have to find out what changed in her life.

"In truth, I do not remember these things. I wrote them in my dream journal. I have always been a vivid dreamer. Almost everyone in my family is. My brother, Leland, he dreamed even more than I do. Such lovely dreams." Sadness marred her face for a second, then disappeared back into that studied face of cultured politeness. "Even on the medication, I still dream, but I do not, cannot, remember what I dream of." Her dark eyes flittered over my face, seeking something. "I cannot tell you why the symbols or labyrinth frightened me. I regained my composure and continued my day." Her hand, with its neatly trimmed fingernails, petted the smooth fabric of her dressing gown.

Again, I said nothing, but gestured for her to continue. Silence was ever my ally. It did appear that Josephine had a rich fantasy life. Not too unusual in the grand scheme of things. The fact that her family seemed to encourage the fantasy in both of their children *was* unusual. They had clearly spoken of their dreams to each other.

Josephine's eyes glazed as she looked into the past. "I thought it was a singular folly. Instead, I woke up screaming the next morning, and the next and the next, for a full week. I did not remember these dreams upon waking. I forced myself to forget them. I did not want to remember." She paused. "Part of me did. But I was too afraid to uncover what made me scream my throat raw each night.

"Two weeks ago, the wounds began to appear on my back. First one symbol—a word, perhaps. Then what I presume was a sentence, to now what you just saw: the paragraph carved into my flesh. I chose to come here for help. I chose you to help me after I discovered you worked here."

"How did you discover this?" I noted Josephine had begun to weave me into her narrative. She assumed I believed the wounds to be writing. Alternatively, she was not willing to accept that I did not believe the wounds to be writing.

"Dr. Mintz mentioned you in passing to Nurse Heather. I remembered your name from Malachi." Josephine gave me a sly smile. "As I am here voluntarily, I still have a say in who treats me. I suspect the good doctor is unhappy with this turn of events."

Again, I suppressed my distaste at the "good" doctor's experiments. "I would not doubt it. Do you mind, though, if I talk to him about his findings?" I wondered if Josephine had mentioned Malachi—*her* Malachi, not mine—to Dr. Mintz. It was a name he would know.

No. It was a coincidence. Nothing more. The name, while not popular, was not unusual. She was not referring to my lost patient.

Josephine shook her head. "No, I do not mind. But I will not be subject to his experiments. I have seen the results in some of his patients as the poor creatures pass by my room."

"Of course." I considered my words carefully. I did not want to agree or disagree with her. Nor did I want to slam any doors. Trust was still being established. I needed to make certain I understood what she was telling me. A clinical summary would be the baseline for future discussions. "As I understand it, for three weeks you have had nightmares, but no memory of what they are about. Is that correct?"

Josephine took a moment to consider my words before she nodded her agreement.

"Two weeks ago, the wounds began to appear. Were they always on your back?"

"No. The first one was on my side." She touched her left hip. "It was a single mark. After that, they moved to my back."

"Do they heal?" I wanted to write out notes, but writing anything down would throw a barrier between us. I would go from confidant to doctor with a single stroke of the pen. Trust, once broken, is difficult to re-establish. I had to rely upon my memory for now.

"Some. Though, they are renewed each night. I fear I will ever carry their scars."

"Has anything new appeared in the last couple of days?" If they had, it would mean her illness was still progressing. If not, it had stabilized…perhaps with the knowledge I would be her new doctor.

Josephine shook her head. "Not that I know of. But my back is so filled with the writing, I would not be able to tell if there were something new. The pain is the same: a single, widespread ache over my entire back, heightened into sharp clarity when fabric is pulled from it."

I held my chin for a moment, considering. As a doctor of the mind, I did not physically examine my patients unless it was absolutely necessary. In this case, I believed it was. I had to see the wounds themselves to mark them and determine their healing progress. It would also give me a better sense of what could have caused them to appear in the first place.

Decided, I stood. "Miss Ruggles, I need to see your wounds. I also need to make a written copy and an impression of them. Will you allow this?"

"What will you do with them?"

"I will not know until I have seen them. It matters how the wounds were made. Looking at them will tell me." I left the door open for Josephine's remarks about her wounds to be true. I also allowed her the dignity to deny me and to protect her fabrications.

While I did not state I thought they were self-inflicted, I watched as disappointment, fear, determination, and acceptance crossed Josephine's face, one after the other. She had decided that I did not believe her, but she felt my examination would vindicate her belief that her dreams caused the marks—that she had not created them herself.

I, on the other hand, expected to see what I have always seen— the torn skin of self-inflicted wounds made by fingernails. It did not matter how neat they were.

Josephine inclined her head. "I will allow this. My maid is waiting outside your office."

Hanna, Josephine's maid, was a lady's maid in every sense. She wore a black dress of good quality and a white apron. Her sepia skin was clear and clean. Her hair—black with grey shot through it—was pulled back into a neat bun. Smile lines graced her face and she did not have the calluses of a maid of all work. Instead, Josephine appeared to be her singular priority.

The two women were comfortable with each other and their respective roles to the point of a heightened, silent language. They understood each other on a level few reached. Hanna would go to the ends of the earth for her mistress, no doubt. Perhaps I could arrange a meeting between the two of us to see if there was something the servant could tell me that the patient could not.

I locked the office door as Hanna helped Josephine with her dress. It was rare for anyone to interrupt me during a session, but it did happen. I wanted no mistakes.

A hiss behind me caught my attention. Turning, I saw Hanna peel the linen cloth from Josephine's back. The maid reached for a soft cloth from the basket she had carried in with her—another foresight of the young Miss Ruggles no doubt. I raised a hand and my voice. "Wait. Please. Allow me to look first."

Hanna glanced at Josephine who nodded her permission. "Pardon, ma'am. I usually bind her wounds each morning. Except for this morning."

At first glance, Josephine's back was a bloody mess, then the marks became clear. I peered close, focusing in on one of the wounds. Her skin puckered outward, as if the mark had been pushed *out* of her rather than scratched *into* her. As I stared, the wound became a glyph before my eyes. Then the rows of marks became sentences. It *was* writing. I felt myself drawn into them. It was familiar and alien at the same time.

"Well?" Josephine asked.

I shook off the train of thought I had followed and focused back to my task. How could I have thought it was writing? They were nothing more than rows of wounds—not glyphs. I needed to determine how the wounds were made. "One moment, please."

When one scratched at a wound over and over, it left a divot. I had patients who had picked their scabs bloody. The edges of those wounds also stood up. However, the edges always morphed with the healing process and the damage caused by the tearing of scab from skin.

These edges were straight and unmarred. I touched a fingertip to Josephine's back, running it over one of the marks. Drying blood rasped against my fingertip, but the flesh beneath was soft. It felt as if this was the first time the wound had been made, even though the lacerations had been there for more than a week. This was not the repeated ripping of skin. This should not be possible.

"If you would, Hanna, clean each wound one at a time. I will copy it down. Then go on to the next one."

"Yes, Doctor."

"Miss Ruggles—"

"Call me Josephine. We are...*intimates*...now. Are we not?"

Though the young woman did not turn around, I sensed her smiling at me, or at a private joke. "As you wish. Josephine, do the wounds continue to weep throughout the day?" I wondered if she noticed I did not invite the same familiarity of having her call me Carolyn. Whether or not she believed we were friends, we were not. There were boundaries we needed to keep as patient and doctor.

"Sometimes. The more difficult the day, the more the wounds react."

"Thank you." I nodded to Hanna. "Begin, please."

We stood like that, the heiress, her maid, and myself: a tableau of concern. Josephine held her dress to her, preserving her modesty. Hanna cleaned each wound one by one and allowed me the time to copy it down exactly before going on to the next one. A heavy silence filled the air—not awkward, just anticipatory.

As Hanna finished cleaning the blood from the last of the marks, more than half of them had begun to glisten and weep. I pulled one of my clean handkerchiefs from a desk drawer and unfolded it. "We will press this to Josephine's back in a single motion," I instructed the maid, "then pull it away as soon as all of the marks show themselves." It would not take long for the fine white cloth to capture the wounds as a whole.

Together, we covered Josephine's back. I pressed a careful hand to the fabric. The glyphs—the wounds—bled through immediately. With a nod, we pulled the handkerchief away, carrying with it a perfect replica of the writing that appeared to force its way out of Josephine's skin.

Something in the way the blood soaked into the cloth pressed another image into my mind: blood forced through the skin in myriad religious paintings. As Hanna bound her mistress's wounds and helped her dress again, one idea crowded my mind: *stigmata*.

Whatever trauma afflicted Josephine's mind, it was possible, logical even, that her only means of expressing that trauma was the manifestation of stigmata-like symptoms. I smiled, relieved. Somehow, I had a possible answer.

But I would need to consult with the "good" Dr. Mintz first.

Chapter 2

After my meeting with Josephine, I sought out her former psycholo-
gist, Dr. Mintz, for any information he would give me. I knew from
the start that this would be a challenge. Thus far, I had refused to link
my research into hypnotic drugs to his research involving his "dream
enhancer." Had I known that his helpfulness was based only on what he
could get from me, I might have refused to work at Arkham Sanatorium.

With this between us, my relationship with the "good" doctor was
strained at best and adversarial at worst. I had hoped to land some-
where in-between in this conversation.

Our meeting went about as well as could be expected.

"Dr. Mintz!" I hailed the doctor just before he disappeared into his
office. He paused in the doorway and waited—a trim, older man
who gazed at me with an air of impatience. He was not a friendly
man when you would not give him what he wanted. While he was
not outright hostile, his pleasant demeanor was saved for those
who were willing to give him something.

"What is it?" He stepped into his office and turned, putting his
hands behind his back.

"Miss Josephine Ruggles. You interviewed her several times.

I thought I would—"

He scoffed, interrupting me. "That hysterical woman? Have you not already sorted out the fact that she is harming herself for attention? Prescribe her some laudanum and send her home."

I paused, taken aback. "Oh? After a week with Miss Ruggles, that is your only diagnosis?"

Dr. Mintz hesitated at my question and the tone of my voice. He *hmphed*. "Well, I must admit, for a woman of her race she is uncommonly well educated, well spoken, and well-to-do. She is remarkable in those rare aspects."

I widened my eyes, hiding my annoyance at his old-fashioned sensibilities. "Her race?"

"Yes. You do not often see black heiresses, or even educated black women for that matter."

"That is not exactly true, Doctor." I kept my voice light. "I come from a well-to-do family. It was required to afford my education. More than one-fourth of my university class was not white. As for well-to-do, when it comes to the *nouveau riche*, which many of the black elite are, it is the color of your money that matters. At least among the younger generation."

The doctor *hmphed* again. "Be that as it may, Dr. Fern, I stand behind my diagnosis of hysteria. Miss Ruggles simply wants attention."

"And her wounds? I have looked at them. They are very regular and the skin around them is—"

"She is talented, I will give her that. Limber enough to scratch all parts of her back. I do not know why she is hurting herself. I did not have enough time to understand that part of her psyche and she would not consent to my treatment." He peered at me, a small, condescending smile played about his lips. "But, if you cannot solve her issues, I would be happy to consult with you. Perhaps it is time we put our collective researches together. It *is* her dreams, she says, that are causing her the distress. If we can get to the root of the problem…"

I shook my head and stepped back. I would find no help here. "No, Doctor. I do not believe that will be necessary. I just wanted to see your private notes from the interviews. Her case file was light on information."

"Private notes are just that, Doctor. Good day." With that, he closed his office door in my face.

I adjusted my glasses. "Thank you for your help," I muttered at the uncaring door. I should have known better. He would not help me unless it also helped him. No wonder the asylum was a depressing place to be. I would need to go to the records room and see if there were something else to be found. Or, better yet, see if I could talk Nurse Heather into dropping a hint of what Dr. Mintz refused to share.

I pulled my suit jacket close. Even here, in the faculty hallway, the permanent chill of the building's stone walls invaded, despite the industrial carpet and the artwork on the walls. It was the only hallway in the entire building to be carpeted. This visual and auditory cue told visitors and patients alike that the top floor of the asylum was not like the rest of it. This was where the doctors had their offices and performed their interviews. Patients in this hallway were always accompanied by asylum staff.

I hurried from the upper hall down the cramped stairwell to the lower floors where Nurse Heather spent most of her time caring for the patients in her own way. The odor of unwashed bodies hit me like a physical blow as I entered the hall. My shoes clacked against the black and white checked floor, stained with dirt and other unmentionable things. Normally, I could ignore the asylum's chill, its smell, and the dim hallway lights that cast unnatural shadows.

I worked here to make it a better place for all—doctors and patients alike. My work was not for the fainthearted, as I had learned during my time at Providence Sanatorium. But I could, and would, continue my work without falling prey to the asylum's air of desperation and damnation. I had to. I seemed to be the only one who would.

It was time to ignore my surroundings and put my task into perspective. This was no different than the first time I walked into a debate or an interview with a recalcitrant patient. It is always the first look that tells me whether or not there will be a problem. Whether it is because I am a woman or younger than whomever I am speaking to, the look is the same. I became an expert at recognizing and ignoring it at the University of Chicago.

• • •

Unsettled or not, by the time I reached the first of the patients' halls, I had my pleasant, professional mask on once more. This was one of the open halls where non-violent patients were allowed to roam between their rooms and the day room. Most days, I saw my patients in their rooms. It made them feel more comfortable. As if they had some control of the situation. I acknowledged Theresa, my dancing patient, when she waved at me—she liked to waltz with the figment of her deceased husband—and Victoria, who sat on the couch and rocked back and forth as if she were a machine. She nodded when she caught my eye, but did not cease her rocking.

I found Nurse Heather escorting an unfamiliar patient back from the showers—one of the few locked doors on this hall. I believe I would recognize the nurse's posture anywhere. With wide shoulders, a rectangular core, and short-cropped, greying hair—impossibly stylish in this austere setting— Nurse Heather would look at home in the latest flapper fashions. She always moved with deliberate intensity, like a woman on a mission. In my mind's eye, I could see her marching in a suffrage protest or dancing at a speakeasy with that same intensity.

Right now, Nurse Heather was focused on moving her patient through the chilly asylum hallway. Behind her, an orderly strolled on patrol, glancing into the patients' rooms. I noted that he kept an eye on Nurse Heather and her patient. The patient seemed common enough. Long, wet, black hair hung in the woman's face, and she had the shuffle of a thoroughly drugged patient. I dismissed her from my mind. She was not my patient, thus not my concern. "Nurse Heather, a word, if I may?"

The older woman gave me an automatic, thin-lipped smile. She held the patient by one arm as she halted in the middle of the hallway. "What is it, Dr. Fern?"

"It is about Josephine Ruggles. I would like Dr. Mintz's files concerning her."

"I'm sure those files were transferred to your office." She gave me a frown and pulled her patient into stillness with an absent gesture. The patient tilted her head toward our conversation.

"Not all of them."

She gave me a look and I worked to keep my breath steady. I could not stop the flush I felt creep up my neck to my cheeks.

"I see. Well then, I guess you need to talk to Dr. Mintz."

"I would, but he is just going to tell me to get them from you. We both know how he is."

She raised her chin to look down her nose at me, suspicion plain on her face. "I'll see—"

The patient, who had been tilting her head up to look at me from beneath her wet hair, moved with sudden speed, pulling herself from Nurse Heather's grasp. She grabbed my arm and yanked us both to our knees. I found myself gazing into a single golden-brown eye, bright as it gave me a gimlet stare. The rest of her face was obscured by her hair.

Before I could pull myself from her, she shook her head, violent and distressed. "You must help her. You're the only one who can."

Startled and stunned, I froze where the patient held me. "Help who?" It was the only thing I could think to say. I tried to get a better look at the woman's face, but she shook her head again, hair still hiding her face. One bright golden-brown eye—lucid despite the drugs in her system—stared back at me.

"It's within her. It was too much for me. Too many things to care for. I couldn't…She needed it…I didn't know what she'd do… the protection failed. You have to help her."

I put my hand on hers, keeping my voice calm. "I do not understand. Whom do I need to help?"

The grip on my arm tightened even as the lucidity in that single eye dimmed and dulled. "Don't make me rip the scales from your eyes. Don't make me. It'll change you forever. It'll change me, too. Please, don't make me do it!"

Then, Nurse Heather had the woman by her shoulders and wrestled her into a standing position. I stood, shaken, and watched the patient. She reached a hand to me. "Help her, please. But don't make me rip the scales from your eyes!" Then, she was in the custody of the orderly. The man wrapped a huge arm about the woman's waist as he bent one of her arms back. He propelled the no-longer-struggling woman before him with ease.

With her free arm, she reached for me, muttering about someone needing help and scales upon eyes. None of it made any sense.

"Put her in her room. Wrap her up until she's calm." Nurse Heather turned and cast an experienced eye up and down me.

"Well, that was interesting. She hasn't said that much at one go since she arrived three weeks ago."

I still felt the patient's grip on my arm, still felt the urgency in her voice, still saw her trap me with her gaze. "Who is she?"

"Professor Sati Das. A professor of archaeology from England. Born in Assam, India to a British father and an Assamese woman. She fell into a coma while visiting some place here on the East Coast. She transferred in from Saint Mary's after she woke and would only babble nonsense about shards and tomes."

It made a strange sort of sense. Her British accent had been tinged with a foreigner's timber. "What did she mean by 'rip the scales from my eyes'? Has she said this sort of thing before? And whom does she want people to help?" I held my arm to my body—it still throbbed with the patient's strength of purpose.

"I don't know the answers to your questions. She's never said such to me." The nurse gave my arm a cursory look, manipulating my wrist, then my elbow. "You're fine. You're going to bruise, but that's all." Nurse Heather adjusted her nurse's cap. "It's strange. She's usually so calm."

I rubbed my arm, trying to banish the feel of Sati's cold hand from it. "Probably the malady she suffers from. We have never seen each other before. Who is her doctor?"

"Dr. Mintz is in charge of her treatment. She's a possible candidate for his dream enhancer." Nurse Heather gazed at me. "I'll have to tell him of her reaction to you—when I get those records you want."

I nodded, knowing that Dr. Mintz would deny the nurse. Or give her copies of the useless information he had already sent over. "Of course."

"Perhaps it's something about you...your hair color or your glasses...that struck such a chord in her." The head nurse continued to peer at me as if I were an interesting bug.

"Perhaps," I agreed, suppressing a shudder. "Thank you for getting those files for me." I gave her a nod and turned on my heel. Nurse Heather did not stop me as I hurried away, although I felt her keen gaze on my back. What else she was going to tell the good doctor about the strange encounter?

Returning to the safety of my office, grateful for the scant warmth within and the familiarity of my books, I was torn between my current case and the encounter with the professor. Why had she reacted so?

Shaking my head to clear it of the patient who was not mine, I turned to my notes of Josephine Ruggles. I peered at the copy I had made of the wounds and compared them with the handkerchief impression. The marks on Josephine's back—they looked so near to writing. Perhaps a cross between Sanskrit and Arabic; something old. A forgotten dialect? Was it possible to have a case of stigmata that resulted in written words on the skin?

I had too many questions and no answers.

In the meantime, I had to consider my treatment of Josephine for her nightmares. Whether the wounds were self-inflicted or stigmata-like symptoms, it was possible, probable even, that she would respond to my hypnotic sessions. The root of her problem was within her mind. I was sure of this.

Ransacking my reference books, I found only one mention of non-Christian-based stigmata—bleeding from the scalp, palms, side, and/or wrists—in a much older, non-medical book from the early 1800s. It was obvious that I would not find such a book in the small asylum reference library; I would need to go to the university library for a chance to find it, or something comparable.

It had been a while since I visited the Orne Library. Perhaps it held the key to Josephine's malady.

Chapter 3

I grew up moving about the United States. My father was a rail man and traveled from station to station, inspecting, improving, and managing them until they met Union Pacific standards. Then, we moved on. The longest we remained in a single location was two years.

This travel allowed me to discover and fall in love with the University of Chicago. One of the more progressive universities when it came to women, I completed my undergraduate work with distinction—and an open mind that many on the East Coast do not possess.

By the time I was ready for my graduate work, my family had settled down in Boston, Massachusetts. This allowed me to choose Pembroke College for my continued studies. I wanted to be close to my family. Throughout my university years, I had occasion to visit the Orne Library at Miskatonic University in search of research material for my thesis.

The University of Chicago has a wonderful library—as does Pembroke College—filled to the brim with books. But it does not have the sensibility, the atmosphere, or the reverence for books that the Orne Library possesses. It is the kind of library bibliotaphs dream of, with its dark woods, huge stacks, and quiet atmosphere.

• • •

Entering Miskatonic University's Orne Library was like walking onto hallowed ground. A preternatural hush lay over the large, open room and the scent of old books permeated the air. Even my steps against the marbled floor were muted. I sighed a happy sigh. This library was home.

My feet knew the way to the card catalog. I slipped through the large wooden tables and nodded to the reference librarian, Ms. Mayer. If I could not find what I wanted, I would ask her. However, the librarian had taught me that I needed to search on my own first because it was likely I would come across something I had not considered before.

My first round of catalog searching did bear fruit, although I was uncertain if any of it would be useful. I had four books to begin with: *Five Wounds: The First Case of Stigmata* by Davidson, 1720; *The Phenomena of Stigmata, Divine and Diabolic* by Spring and Mayhew, 1895; *Stigmata: An Investigation* by Hunt and Mead, 1901; *The Miracle of Stigmata* by Harrington, 1910. Although none of them were medical in nature, they would begin to give me an idea of whether or not Josephine's marks could be from stigmata.

While I was collecting the four books, I chanced upon one called *Written in Blood* by Sutherlin and Drury-Crusett, 1919. It was new and, at first glance, appeared to be far more analytical than the first four books. I added it to my pile. When I returned to the large wooden tables, I found myself choosing what had once been my usual seat—a table in the back corner that gave me a good view of the rest of the room. One that would limit the number of people walking behind me.

As progressive as both my universities were, that did not stop some of the less enlightened of my peers from "pranking" the women of my class. Twice I had water dumped on me from behind while I was in the library doing research, hours of work ruined. Twice I walked back to my room, soaked and flushed with classmates snickering behind my back. Twice was enough. I learned to sit where I could watch the room, the people, and my back.

Hours later, I had pages of notes on stigmata, but I was not sure if any of it would assist me with Josephine. There were no cases of stigmata appearing while the sufferer slept. There were no cases, or even stories, of the stigmata wounds spelling out words in any language. Not even stories of stigmata making a design within the flesh.

All of the research—if you could call it that—was steeped in religious mysticism and always led back to the Christ figure. Even the promising *Written in Blood* book came up empty with the exception of referencing another book, *Anomalistic Thinking in Regards to Miracles* by Avi Zunger, a Jewish scholar. There was no date given for the book and I could not find it in the card catalog.

It was time to see Ms. Mayer.

I approached the reference desk with the same quiet reverence one gives respected professors. A librarian is the caretaker of the books and knows their secrets. Treat both well, and you will be rewarded with knowledge. That was what I needed now.

Ms. Mayer was an older woman; her thick hair, held at the nape of her neck in a chignon, was more grey than black. She wore an impeccable polka-dotted dress and a sweater. She also had reading glasses on a long chain about her neck.

Ms. Mayer waited until I was at the reference desk to look up. Her eyes brightened with familiarity. "Miss Fern, I saw you come in. Is it 'Doctor' now?"

"Doctor," I confirmed.

"Well done."

"Thank you."

"What may I do for you?"

"I am looking for this book." I showed her the book's name and author. "However, it does not seem to be in the card catalog. It was mentioned in another book as reference material for the psychology behind miracles and magical thinking in regards to stigmata."

The librarian looked away for a long, silent moment, consulting her mental card catalog. She nodded to herself. "If we have it, there are a couple of places it could be. I won't be long."

With that, she left me at the reference desk. I knew better than to follow her around like a lost puppy. Instead, I returned the books I pulled to their rightful places within the stacks. I also gathered up my things. Either Ms. Mayer would find what I needed or I would be done here.

By the time I returned to the reference desk, the librarian was waiting for me. She was bent over a large tome of handwritten notes—a ledger, perhaps, or a manifest. I waited quietly until she straightened. "This is an interesting book you've requested. It's in the Rare Book Room."

"I see. Will I be allowed to look at it?" I was not certain. As one of the visiting staff from the asylum, I was permitted some access to the library, but I was not sure what privileges that afforded me.

Ms. Mayer nodded. "Yes, but you will be required to stay within the Rare Book Room and to use cotton gloves. I trust you have some?"

"Yes, ma'am. I do." I showed her my gloved hands. I had kept the habit of storing cotton gloves, along with my usual gloves, in my handbag at all times—a holdover from spending many hours working with pen and paper at the university. Of course, I wore gloves outside of the asylum, but such formality was not needed within it.

She wrote something on a note card. "The Rare Book Room is on the second floor to your left at the end of the hallway. Keep that card with you. It is both reference and…" she gave me a knowing smile, "…a permission slip to be in the room. You will find what you seek on the third bookcase, the second shelf. While it isn't particularly old, it is rare and fragile. Do be careful."

I knew the admonishment was automatic. "Of course. Thank you for your help."

"You're welcome. Remember that the library closes at seven tonight, sharp."

"I shall remember." As I turned toward the stairs, I glanced at my watch. It was already just past five. I had been here for hours without realizing how much time had passed. That was the way research was. But my patient list was light and my duties would continue in the morning. For now, I was on the trail of something that might help my newest patient.

At the end of the second-floor hallway stood an imposing set of double doors. Above the doors, a sign proclaimed this to be the *Ruggles Rare Book Room*. To the side of the closed doors, a gold and black plaque hung at eye level. I approached it with wary curiosity.

Dedicated to Thomas Ruggles (1846–1918)
In honor of his dedication to the printed word and his
lifelong commitment *to spreading knowledge to one and*

all. In remembrance of his generous support to the Orne Library. A man faithful to his family, friends, and community. His loss reminds us how important it is for the librarian to guide the novice, transmit culture, and provide information in times of chaos. He will be missed.
In loving memory, Alonzo and Nina Ruggles

I touched the raised bronze letters of the last two names. Alonzo and Nina were the names of Josephine's parents. At first blush, it appeared to be an unbelievable coincidence. Then I remembered that Josephine was the heiress to the Ruggles Publishing fortune. Of course her grandfather—if that was who Thomas Ruggles was—and her parents supported the university and its library.

I opened the doors to the Rare Book Room and took a breath, looking around. Rather than the greys and whites and dark wood of the lower floor, this room was decorated in lighter shades of brown and beige. I turned up the lights. Heavy russet drapes blocked all natural light from the delicate books. The temperature was cool but dry. I closed the doors to preserve the climate.

Ochre bookcases with glass fronts lined the walls with two sets of standing shelves that stood alongside three large tables. Each set of shelves had a brass number on top of it. So much esoteric knowledge. It made my head spin. Even the floor was mixture of light and dark woods in a spiraling pattern; a striking contrast to the lower level's marble floor.

Knowing that time was of the essence, I moved to the third bookcase and opened the glass doors. Each of them could be locked, it seemed, and I wondered if the librarians locked the shelves or just the Rare Book Room door at night. The unmistakable scent of antique books greeted me like an old friend. Even as I scanned the second shelf for the book I wanted, I noticed that there was no dust. The librarians tended this room, and its valuable contents, well.

My treasure found, I settled in at one of the tables to read.

Anomalistic Thinking in Regards to Miracles by Avi Zunger had been written in Hebrew and translated into English. Most likely, this had been a student's graduate project. Written from back to front, a page of neatly typed English translation had been stuck between the book's pages with marks of corresponding work in the original writing. The student had probably been a linguistic major rather than a philosophy or psychology student.

I dug into the text. Avi Zunger had an interesting way of explaining the mental calisthenics the mind went through to accept the impossible. While a child could accept everything presented, no matter how improbable, Zunger questioned what could cause an adult to do the same. Perhaps there was a bound translation of the book I could order. It would be an expensive indulgence, but this book belonged in my personal library as valuable reference material.

Even as the minutes ticked by and I wrote out notes to consider when approaching Josephine and her wounds, I wondered if I had accepted the idea of stigmata too easily. I rolled this idea over and over in my mind as I gazed at the floor. Something about it was familiar…and alien.

My vision blurred. I'd stopped taking notes, stopped reading the text. The wooden pattern spiraled and undulated as if alive. The darker russet brown shapes morphed and flowed through the wood in a way not dissimilar to the marks on Josephine's back.

I pulled the note of the three symbols I'd scrawled as reference from my handbag and held it up just left of my eyes. As I compared the design of the floor to the symbols, I let my eyes relax. The marks on the floor and my note blurred in the same manner, almost becoming one design.

Was this room somehow related to my patient's malady?

I considered the answer as I put the paper away. Of course Josephine would have seen this room when it was dedicated to her family member. Of course it would have affected her. Was all this a delayed response of grief to her grandfather's passing? I would have to talk to her about this. What *had* her relationship been with Thomas Ruggles? And why would it have taken more than two years for the grief to manifest in such an overt and bloody manner?

Checking my watch, I saw it was already half past six. I needed to clean up and bid Ms. Mayer a good evening. Perhaps she would know who the designer of this room was, and I would be able to link the marks on Josephine's back to her grandfather through the designer.

Chapter 4

Hypnotic therapy is not for all my patients. Many are too untrusting, temperamental, or are unwilling to relax enough to explore their inner thoughts through the guided technique. For a patient like that, I use a more standard set of psychological tools to get to the heart of their malady—if it is possible.

My hypnotic therapy technique came about after much research and thought. The essence of the matter is that many patients cannot face their trauma in the cold, hard light of day. But, in a relaxed, sleepy, hypnotic state, the inner child (or critic) loosens its hold and allows them to examine their trauma with a more objective mind.

I was fortunate that the chemist at Providence Sanatorium was willing to converse with me and come up with the concoction that I use today. The sedative relaxes both the body and the mind without causing blackouts. It is enough to still the discomfort of those unable to relax and open the mind to suggestion, allowing the patient to be led down difficult paths to examine their own fear and trauma. They remain just conscious enough to be aware of me, my guiding authority, and my representation of safety.

This is what I had decided Josephine needed. I was right.

• • •

With the sun high in the sky, Josephine was the last of my patients I was to see today. I pulled the drapes closed as Josephine settled in. She looked as neat as she had yesterday, in a pale blue dress and a sweater, but the hollows beneath her eyes were deeper, darker, and more haunted. She watched me with a curious gaze, but said nothing. I had to prompt her into conversation again. "How are you?"

"Did I have the nightmare last night? Yes. Did I bleed again? Yes. Am I in pain? No. No more than usual." The heiress gestured to the room. "The office is set up in a different manner than yesterday."

I knew she referred to the sitting area of the office in specific. Her abrupt manner and immediate change of topic said just how bad last night had been. Weary and wary, Josephine hurt.

"Yes. The setup is new for you, but this is how I arrange things for almost all my hypnotherapy sessions. It is a visual cue for your subconscious as much as it is for comfort and utility."

The two overstuffed armchairs sat across from each other with the coffee table just to the side. The low table held my papers from her file, my examination notes, and the library research. The sedative I liked to use—syringe and drug bottle—sat on top of it all next to my light enhancer.

I sat down across from her. We were very close, with our knees no more than a couple handbreadths apart. This closeness inspired trust and honesty for some patients like Josephine. Others, I had to sit much farther away. "After some careful thought, I have some ideas about your case. Have you experienced anything tragic in the last couple of years? A loss, perhaps?"

Josephine considered this for a long moment. "I have had losses, yes…though, I cannot think of anything I would consider tragic."

"The loss of a family member or a childhood friend?"

She shook her head. "Not in the last couple of years."

Repression was a natural reaction to the pain of losing a loved one. It is not unusual for my patients to be unaware of both their loss and the mark it left on their psyche. "I believe your wounds may be a unique case of stigmata-like symptoms born of grief."

Josephine watched me, waiting for me to elaborate. When I did not, her rigid posture relaxed. "Grief? What am I…who am I grieving for?"

"Grief," I confirmed. "We will speak of that soon."

Her face shifted from confusion to surprise and grateful relief. "You believe me? I didn't…. That I did not harm myself?"

"I believe you." Josephine had dismissed the idea she was suffering from grief because I might actually believe her. This relief and gratitude would make her much more amenable to our hypnotherapy session. I would need to use this.

Another note of interest. Until this moment, she had not used a contraction with me. Perhaps it was a sign of high emotion. I would watch for it and determine its trigger. Unconscious mannerisms rarely lied—even when the patient was guarded. I gave myself a mental note to notice any and all contractions she used.

Josephine closed her eyes. "Thank you."

"You are aware I use hypnotherapy with my patients to get to the roots of their problems."

She nodded.

"I would like to use this technique on you."

"What does it require?" Suspicion returned to her voice and stiffened her posture as she opened her eyes once more. "What will it feel like? It sounds…unusual."

"It *is* unusual. Odd and strange. Some of my colleagues have called me crazy. However, they cannot deny my results or my number of cured patients." I shrugged. "It requires nothing from you except your willingness to proceed. You cannot hypnotize a person who does not wish to be. They must be willing." I gestured to the syringe and bottle of clear liquid. "This is a sedative. Again, it is not required, but it does relax the patient and make them more willing to go on the hypnotic journey."

"If I do this, what will we do?"

"We will journey into your mind. We will find the source of your pain."

Josephine locked eyes with me. "You will be with me?" It was a question, a plea, and on the outside edges, it was a command. She was a woman used to being obeyed.

"I will be with you the entire time. I'll not leave your side."

"My mind is a dangerous place, if my nightmares are any indication."

It was a challenge. I nodded. "That may well be, but I will not leave your side while we are in session. You are safe with me." This was a promise I gave all my patients and I held my promises dear.

Her smile was brittle. "I do not believe that is true, Doctor, but I believe you are sincere." With that, she unbuttoned the cuff of one sleeve and pushed both the sweater and linen fabric up, exposing her forearm. She offered it to me.

I didn't hesitate. I prepared the sedative and administered it. All the while, I spoke: part distraction, part information. "In my research, I came across a scholar who investigated the way the mind reacted when presented with the impossible—miracles, magic, the supernatural. When we are young, we accept these things because we don't know that we shouldn't. The same thing happens in dreams. When we are older and we are presented with such, we reject it until we have no other explanation. In dreams, we revert to a childlike state of acceptance of the impossible because our minds do not let us know it is impossible."

"This is what the hypnotherapy will do?"

"Yes." I pressed a cotton ball to the injection site before covering it with a bandage. I even helped her straighten her sleeve and button her cuff, as if I were a stand-in for Hanna. "If we are expecting something miraculous to occur, it is as if our minds regress to an innocent state of acceptance. Thus, when the event happens, we accept it without question."

I dimmed the lights until one light shone above and behind Josephine. "This is what I want you to do. I want you to acknowledge and accept every thought that comes to your head as we journey. No matter what you think, you will be safe. I shall be by your side."

"Do you promise?" Josephine's voice already had the soft quality of one relaxed.

I saw her slump against the comfortable chair. Her dark brown eyes watched me from under heavy lids. "I promise. I won't leave your side while we're in session." I picked up the light enhancer from the coffee table—a device I had invented to help my patients go under. It was little more than a wooden frame with a metal disk suspended in the middle by a thin wire. I sat down across from her. "Focus your attention here, on this disk, Josephine." I set the disk rocking back and forth. The moving light played over her face.

Josephine smiled. "No watch?"

"No watch," I confirmed. "This is therapy, not a sideshow act. No need for a flashy watch to catch the eyes of both an audience and a participant. Just this. Just you. Just me. Focus on this light and let your thoughts wander. Let them go where they will. If your eyelids are heavy, let them close."

She closed her eyes, opened them once, and then closed them again.

I kept my voice low and smooth. A consistent monotone was the key until the patient was under. "Remember, you are safe with me."

"Safe." Josephine's voice was soft and asleep. The sedative mixture worked quickly.

I lowered the light enhancer to my lap. "We are going on a journey. I want you to think about the last three weeks. Think about them as if they happened to someone else. There is a sheer veil between you and the memories. When you remember, it will be as if it happened to someone else. They cannot touch you. Do you understand, Josephine?"

"It cannot touch me." Her chest rose and fell in regular, slow breaths. Calm and serene.

"Go deeper, Josephine. Sleep. Let your thoughts take you where they will." When Josephine did not respond, I waited and counted her slow breaths. On her seventh breath I asked, "Josephine? Can you hear me?"

"Yes." Her answer was an exhale of breath.

"We have begun your journey. Where are you?"

"I'm approaching the Seventy Steps of Light Slumber."

I paused. That was a peculiar turn of phrase I had never heard before. It seemed specific and important to Josephine. "Describe where you are. Tell me about the Seventy Steps of Light Slumber."

"I walk the path of stone toward the stairs. On either side of me is the mist. I can hear things in it."

I watched Josephine's face. She appeared more than just relaxed. She was comfortable with her surroundings. "How do you feel?"

"I feel fine, thank you." The response was automatic. "I know this place. I have been here before." Josephine paused for a long time, her head twitching back and forth. "Where are you?"

"I am right here, Josephine. Right by your side."

"Not there. I need you *here*. You promised. The Stairs are just down the path. I need you *with* me."

My frown matched hers. I didn't understand. I put the light enhancer on the table and reached out to cover one of her hands with my own. "I'm right here, Josephine."

She flipped her hand over and grabbed me by the wrist in a grip stronger than I expected. "There you are. Come. We need to go. There is something I must do."

I winced as the light above Josephine's head shone bright in my face. Then gravity shifted and I was falling through a rainbow of colors. Before I could cry out, my falling body shifted and I was flying. I could see Josephine's hand on my wrist, but nothing else of her. All around me colored light pulsed and shimmered in undulating waves.

Gravity reasserted itself as my head spun and the world tilted sideways. My body, crouched forward as I had been sitting on the edge of the chair, stumbled forward in an effort to keep me from falling. The chair was gone. Josephine grabbed me by the shoulder. It kept me from tumbling to the ground, but not from banging into the hard wall that hadn't been there moments before.

Dazed, I pulled back from my patient and the wall. I stared. I was not in my office anymore. I didn't know where I was. I hugged myself, blinking and gasping, trying to make sense of what had just happened.

We were in a stone corridor without any windows or doors. The air was fresh with a faint tinge of wetness. It reminded me a little of the asylum, but the smell was wrong—wetter, loamier. I looked for the lights, saw none, and wondered how the hallway was illuminated. The walls were cool and moist to the touch. More importantly, they were solid.

It was impossible. The wet chill, so familiar and so different from the normal atmosphere of the asylum, told me otherwise. All my senses told me I was here, in this new, unfamiliar place.

Josephine stood halfway between me and the darkness at the end of the hallway—a hallway that hadn't been there before. One I didn't recognize. "Where are we?"

She tilted her head and gave me the kind of look you give a particularly slow student when the answer is obvious. "The Dreamlands, of course."

I walked to her, noting that she no longer wore a dress. Instead, she wore the kind of thing a working archaeologist might wear in the field—pants, boots, shirt, gloves, belt with canteen, and a vest.

Everything had changed. I was still in my usual work attire—long skirt, blouse, warm suit jacket, stockings, and sensible shoes. I was the same as before. "I don't understand. I, *we*, were in my office."

Josephine let out a slow breath. "We don't have time for this. I have a task to perform."

"What task?" My mind spun, confused. We'd just been in a therapy session in my office. How had we gotten here?

"Once we get down the Stairs." She turned and walked down the corridor.

I rubbed my face and looked again. The stone corridor was still there. I followed her at a slower pace, grappling with this turn of events. Perhaps my foray into anomalous thinking put me into a similar hypnotic state. Perhaps, that was what was needed with Josephine's case. I struggled to put myself back into the doctor's state of mind, to regain my equilibrium.

"Josephine, describe what you see."

She stopped and turned to me. "You see what I see. Don't you?"

"You mentioned mist before. I don't see mist."

"Oh. Well, there is a stone path. It is black and worn, but not dusty. All around us is mist and shadows within the mist. Above, there is a purple sky with blue-purple clouds." She gestured to each area as she spoke. "What do you see?"

I took a slow breath, working hard to remain calm—or to at least appear to be calm. I would not panic. I had my patient's mental state to consider. "I see a long stone corridor that leads into darkness." I pointed down the hallway. "It's cool and damp here. I don't know where the light comes from." I watched her with a keen eye to see what her response would be to the fact that I disagreed with what she said was around us.

Her response was not as I expected.

Josephine laughed and clapped her hands together with delight. "That is the Dreamlands. It is a bit different for everyone. Still, you see the same path I do, leading in the same direction. That is enough for now." She turned away and walked toward the darkness.

The farther she went, the more the darkness receded. I could almost see a door at the end of the hall. As I moved to follow her, a small hand touched my arm. Behind me was a child in tan shorts, white shirt, peach tie, and a tan jacket. He also wore black knee socks and black shoes. "What can I do for you?" I asked.

"You understand that you are making a huge mistake, yes?" The child gave a contemptuous sniff. "That woman is hysterical. If you follow her, you will fall into her delusions."

"Miss Ruggles is my patient, Dr. Mintz. I will do what I believe is best. Right now, it is a joint hypnotherapy session." Eying the spoiled child, part of me understood this version of Dr. Mintz was my subconscious fighting against the surrealistic turn the therapy session had taken. Dr. Mintz was jealous of my skill and my ability to help my patients without torturing them, and so my mind had transformed him into the form of a petulant little boy.

"You will regret this," he warned.

"No, I won't. If you'll excuse me, I'm very busy." I turned from the child and felt the door close behind me. Josephine stood there with a smile.

She gestured before us. "The Seventy Steps of Light Slumber."

Though we had not moved, the corridor was gone. We were on the edge of a cliff at the top of a set of steep stairs. They were wooden and interconnected by stiff wires that kept them still as they hung in the air without a visible means of support. It was a straight line down to an island landing, also suspended in mid-air.

On this landing, there was a huge gate that spanned the width of the rocky platform. Gold-bronze and glimmering, the gate reached skyward and appeared to go on forever, disappearing into a roiling darkness above that reminded me of storm clouds. I looked down and saw the cliff edge we stood on jutted out over nothing. Not darkness. Just nothing. It was all my mind could compare it to. My stomach flip-flopped. I stepped backward.

"Time to go, Doctor." Josephine beckoned before she took to those fragile stairs, the only touchstone above the chasm of nothingness.

I looked down to the landing again. This time, I saw two robed figures—one in red and one in black—standing before the gates. Each held a huge weapon at the ready.

Chapter 5

I have never been one to refuse a challenge. To show weakness or uncertainty in front of my peers in college was to admit weakness— something I could not afford to do in that competitive world. This has served me well in my professional life. Unexpectedly, this stubbornness and unwillingness to acquiesce assisted me in my efforts to learn how to lucid dream. When faced with an impossible situation, I learned to accept what I saw and to seek out specific cues to my state of being—awake or asleep.

Josephine descended the stairs with a grace and surety born of familiarity. I descended at a slower pace, still thinking about how I got here. If I focused on that, I couldn't focus on how high up we were and how small each step was. I was still within my office. But, somehow, I was also in a hypnotic state. This wasn't real. It couldn't be. Was I lucid dreaming? I tested this.

Looking down and to the left, I asked, "Am I awake?" I looked up and around. I was still upon the wooden stairs. I felt awake. I looked at my wristwatch. 3:11. I looked away and at it again. Still 3:11. In dreams, I had never been able to read my watch a second time. Ergo, I was awake. I looked at my blue skirt and thought,

I should be wearing pants. I need pants for an adventure. Before my eyes, my skirt shimmered into pants. Rather than being startled, I relaxed. I *was* in a hypnotic dream state—both dreaming and awake. It accounted for the conflict of visual clues. My will was strong enough to control it if I could just remember the truth of the reality I was now in.

Movement caught my eye. The robed figures below crossed their weapons before Josephine. How had she gotten so far ahead of me? I promised to stay by her side. Heart racing, I descended the stairs faster than was comfortable, almost stumbling. A fall would be disastrous. There was nothing except an endless chasm below. Even as the robed figures straightened and allowed Josephine to pass, I wondered if it was this fall that made people on the edge of sleep jerk awake.

Pushing the thought away, I hurried down the stairs. "Josephine, wait…"

She paused, a beige-clad black woman on the other side of gold barred gates. "You have not been here before. You must show Nasht and Kaman-Thah that you are strong enough to survive the Seven Hundred Steps of Deeper Slumber." Although she was far away, she didn't yell. I could hear her as if she stood by my side.

"How?" I ran in an uneven gait toward them, keeping my eyes on the landing. I refused to look elsewhere.

"You will know." Josephine turned her back to me and waited.

I slowed as I reached the guardians—for they could be nothing else. They were huge, at least twice as tall and twice as wide as a man. Up close, the robes were identical except for the color. Both had similar beards, but I couldn't see their faces. The beards—brown, long, and evenly trimmed, hung to their chests. The hoods that obscured their faces stood irregular from their heads, as if they wore crowns beneath the fabric. They crossed their weapons, a halberd and a scythe, before the gate and remained silent.

I waited, keeping my own silence.

"Time is of the essence." It was Josephine. The words were whispered in my ear even though she had not turned around.

Mustering my courage, I raised my chin. "I will pass. I have a job to do."

In response, each guardian held out a closed fist. "Which hand revives the dead?" Although neither guardian spoke, the voice was all around me. Both robed figures opened their fists just long enough for me to see a crushed butterfly within before closing them again.

I bowed my head in thought. It was a test. One of mental fortitude. It was a trick as well. It had to be. Some part of my subconscious created this challenge to show me how difficult Josephine's case would be and to prove to her that I was up to the challenge.

I concentrated and held out two closed fists as I raised my head. "These hands revive the dead." With that, I opened my hands and released two butterflies—both very much alive.

The guardians, Nasht and Kaman-Thah, opened empty hands before they straightened their weapons and allowed me access to the gate. Holding my breath, I approached and pulled on the gold bars. The gates didn't move. They seemed rooted deep within the rock. I peered close. Glimmering, gold, and just far enough apart that I should be able to slide through them.

As Josephine said, time was of the essence—perhaps she feared that the longer she spent in the asylum, the more likely Dr. Mintz would turn her into one of his experimental subjects. I pushed through the bars. It was tight, but they bowed, allowing me to pass.

Josephine waited at the head of another impossibly steep set of stairs that had no rail and disappeared into the darkness below. They looked exactly like the stairs I'd already traversed. I didn't want to go down another set of stairs like that again. I looked back at the gate. The bars were tightly spaced. I shouldn't have been able to fit through there. My mind gnawed on this.

Josephine touched my arm. "We must go."

"Where?"

She nodded down the steps that terrified me. "The Seven Hundred Steps of Deeper Slumber. At the bottom, we will reach the Enchanted Wood."

Josephine continued to improve. Her cheeks flushed with exhilaration and the darkness beneath her eyes had all but disappeared. Her speech had returned to its normal formality. "How do you know this?"

Josephine shrugged as she looked around. "I have been here before. This is the beginning of every journey."

"Tell me what you see."

She glanced at my face, searching for something, before she turned to our surroundings. "The stairs spiral down. They are marble. The handrail is wrought iron. All around us the sun shines and puffy clouds drift through. Within the clouds, pupperflies play."

As she spoke, I imagined what she described. Before my eyes, the straight, deeply plunging stairs became a marble spiral with a wrought iron handrail. They reminded me of the marble stairs within the university library. I seized upon this and focused to make the stairs I saw match the stairs I was familiar with. As I did so, the encroaching darkness receded and fluffy clouds appeared. I didn't see anything playing within the clouds, and I didn't know what "pupperflies" were, thus they weren't important.

What was important was the fact that this was a shared dream-state hallucination—mostly. As long as the two of us agreed upon what we saw, all would be well. It would make for a fascinating research paper in the future. I gestured for her to go ahead. "Lead on. This is your adventure."

Josephine hesitated before beginning her descent. "You believe me? You see what I see?"

"I forced my mind to see as you see. For me, so many stairs is dangerous. But as you said, you've been here before. I knew they wouldn't seem dangerous to you. I needed to see things the way you see them. Does that make sense?" I followed her, keeping close behind. The iron railing was a comfort and I kept my hand on the cool metal. It was not the wood of the university library staircase, but it was a banister and that was worth everything. This control meant I could continue on and help Josephine like I had been unable to help Malachi.

"Is that part of your anomalous thinking?"

"A little. I'm not in a childlike state, but I am willing to entertain what comes to your mind."

We both laughed at that. Our laughter trailed off at a sound. Josephine and I stopped on the stairs and listened. For a long moment, we could only hear our own breath. Then it came again: a cry for help.

Josephine gasped, "Oh no! I forgot. How could I do that? I'm late. Oh, poor kitty."

Without waiting for me, Josephine sprinted down the winding

staircase. Whatever was happening was bad. She'd lost control and used contractions again. I ran after her, slower and less sure, but sped up as another cry for help came from below.

I fell just as Josephine disappeared from view.

Tumbling down the stairs, I banged against the railing and rebounded, rolling over and over. My head struck the corner of a marble stair. Lights flashed before me. The pain was enormous. Dazed, I continued to fall. It was too much. I was about to go over the railing. If I did that, I would fall to my death. Or worse, I'd never stop falling.

As I bounced up and over the railing, I shot out a hand and grabbed for whatever I could. I caught one of the balusters and slid down it. My body jerked as I hit the bottom rail and held on. I hung there—partly suspended over nothing and partly over the winding staircase. I could try to climb up or try to swing myself over the stairs below and drop. I wasn't strong enough for the former, and the latter gave me a chance of falling into the abyss.

I looked down. The stairs were so far away. I closed my eyes. "This is a dream. This isn't real. I can fly. I can fly." I swung my legs back and forth and opened my eyes as I flung myself at the stairs. "I can fly!"

I didn't fly.

I didn't fall.

I floated from my hanging spot to the stairs I'd been looking at. As I landed with a soft bump, I collapsed to my knees and shuddered. I was much closer to the bottom than I had been, but I needed to collect myself. I covered my face, shaking, and forced slow, calming breaths.

There was no time for that.

As Josephine's shouts entered the fray from below, I remembered why I was here: I *needed* to be by my patient's side. Josephine would not be another Malachi. She would not die under mysterious circumstances. With a speed and agility borne by my sense of duty, I was up and sprinting down the last of the stairs once more. This time, there was no hesitation, no fear. My patient needed me. I would be there for her.

The bottom of the stairs disappeared into the deep, green foliage of oak leaves and trees. I didn't pause. I plunged into, then through, the branches that wound themselves around the stairs. I met the ground with enough give that I was forced to stop and get my bearings. It was the loamy soil of a deep forest, covered in years of fallen leaves that hid gnarled roots and ankle-breaking holes.

I pushed myself to my knees. All around me, glowing fungi dotted the forest floor. This must be the Enchanted Wood. Things rustled in the underbrush as I looked for Josephine—things I didn't want to see. Some of the oak trees appeared to be fighting vines that threatened to strangle them. As I watched, a vine shifted and slithered around a thick branch as if it was alive, sentient. Shouts broke through my horrified fascination.

Two voices rose above the squeaks and chatter of animals. Josephine shouted, "Get away! Get away from him!" The other voice, higher pitched like a child's, encouraged her. "Get 'em, Josephine! Get 'em!"

I surged to my feet and ran in the direction of the melee. I hurried as fast as I could through the unfamiliar forest. I dodged around oak trees with branches that had exploded out from their trunks like frozen fireworks in wood. I rounded a large tree and stumbled into a glade. In the middle was the largest oak tree I'd even seen. Josephine, standing on its jutting roots, was dwarfed by the size of them. Above her was an orange cat. Below her was a swarm of creatures I'd never seen before. They looked like a cross between a rat and a weasel, with large, tattered ears, bulbous, goat-like eyes, and a writhing mass of tentacles where their mouths should be.

As they leapt for Josephine with sharp claws and grasping tentacles, they chattered and squeaked to each other. As one, they would leap upon the oaken roots to dart at Josephine's feet. She swung her makeshift weapon, a fallen branch, forcing them back again.

I saw a small contingent of the creatures move with silent steps around the huge tree to the back. They climbed with slow, sinuous motions, flat against the bark. Their target was the orange cat.

I needed a weapon. A good one. One I was familiar with. I saw it in my mind's eye. My father's 1911 Colt .45. Not a decade before, he'd carried it in the Great War. When I started at Providence, he forced me to learn to shoot, and learn I did. I was very good. The pistol now resided in my office desk in the back of one of the drawers. I'd never used it on the job, but I still kept in practice.

Even as I thought about the pistol, I felt its weight in my hand. It was a comfort. I didn't need to look down to know it was there. I braced my arm against a branch and aimed. The shot went wide of the tree. I instinctually knew I shouldn't hurt the creature I'd aimed at. The shot was deafening in the forest and every single creature froze at its sound.

Coming out from behind the tree, I called in a loud, strong voice. "I am very good with this pistol. I didn't hit any of you on purpose. It's time for you to go. Now." I don't know why I spoke to those creatures as I did, but they'd displayed intelligence. I assumed they'd understand me.

They did.

As one, they swarmed toward me—not in malice, but curiosity. A tumble of voices cascaded around me. "Who is she?" "She's new." "She has a weapon. A strong weapon." "A good ally."

I stood my ground. They stopped about ten feet from me in a clump. One of them came forward and peered with those disconcerting, goat-like eyes. "You didn't hurt us. Why?"

I shook my head. "I didn't have to." This close up I could see their tentacles had suckers on them and wondered how they could eat, and what. I refused to think about what they would've done to the cat.

"You are good and strong. Come. Come with the zoog. We're good allies. Come now. The Enchanted Wood is dangerous. We'll protect you."

Again, I shook my head and sheathed the pistol in the thigh holster I knew was there. "No. I have other duties. Thank you." I glanced up at Josephine. At this point, she was on the ground next to the oak tree with the orange cat wrapped about her shoulders.

The zoog began muttering and chittering among themselves. "As you will. The cats of Ulthar are dangerous. When they betray you, come back here. Come to us. We'll protect you."

I inclined my head once—an acknowledgment, but not an agreement—and said nothing. They looked between us a last time, then scampered off as one into the forest like a moving carpet of fur, tentacles, and claws. As they went, I hurried to Josephine.

"That was brilliant." The words came from the orange cat wrapped about Josephine's shoulders.

"A talking cat. Can this get any weirder?" I shook my head. "Are you all right?"

Josephine smiled at me as she nodded. "Absolutely. It will get much weirder. It *is* the Dreamlands after all. Also, yes, I am well." She pet the cat that snuggled to her. "This is Foolishness, a friend of mine."

"Foolishness. A pleasure." I started to offer a hand, but I didn't know what the etiquette of meeting a talking cat was. I settled for crossing my arms. "What are you doing out here?"

The cat yawned. "I do what I'm supposed to do. I'm foolish. I walk in the Enchanted Wood alone. I get harried by the zoog. You, or someone like you, rescues me. We all have our parts to play in keeping the Dreamlands as stable as it can be."

I looked around the glade and at the huge oak tree in front of us. The world looked stable enough. Grass peeked up through the fallen leaves. Tiny flowers made of colored paper adorned the winding tree roots that edged the glade. The sun shone overhead. It even looked as if some of the trees were smiling.

Foolishness stood on Josephine's shoulders, stretched, then jumped down. "Come along. I'm sure you wish to speak to Insightful. She'll know what you're doing here." With that he strode off toward a path through the forest I hadn't noticed before.

Josephine linked an arm through mine and led me down the open road. Flowers appeared at our sides as we passed by. "I love that kitty. He is his namesake, but he is an ally."

"You know him?" The trees above us made a natural tunnel of green and gold at the top that morphed into a darkness filled with fungi and scuttling creatures at the bottom. I kept my eyes and attention on the orange cat strutting in front of us with his tail held high.

"Oh, yes. I've rescued him dozens of times."

"Have you ever failed to rescue him?" Josephine didn't respond, but from the look on her face the answer was yes.

Ahead, the forest thinned and ended as tree branches parted, allowing us passage. We stopped at the tree line. Josephine gave a grand gesture as if she were revealing something magnificent. In truth, she was. Across a field, I saw the first buildings of Ulthar.

Chapter 6

When you move every couple of years, as I did when I was young, you learn that places are different. Not just strange people and new buildings. It is the landscape itself. The color palette is subtly off until you get used to it. Trees are the wrong shade of green and are shaped differently—rounder instead of triangular. The grass is lighter or longer or stiffer. The buildings are made from yellower rock instead of red. It seemed to me that the farther away from the coast you went, the lighter, yellower, or browner the landscape became. If you were not looking for it, all you would know is that something was "not right" about the new place you were in.

One of the things I would do as a child when we arrived at our new home was pick out exactly what was different—flora, fauna, and colors. I did not know it then, but I was creating coping mechanisms for the loss of my home and friends and all things familiar.

At first, it looked like a small New England village, but the closer we came, the more it looked like what someone *thought* a New England village should look like. Between the meadow and the start of the village was a road that gave Ulthar the perfect border. The rest of the village was displayed like a postcard on the gentle slope of the foothills. The village proper clustered together in a series of business buildings and homes. The rest of the land to either side of the village was farmland as far as the eye could see. Behind it all, the mountain stood as if shepherding its flock below.

It was beautiful and not quite right. It was too neat, too properly quaint for a real village. The central area appeared to be laid out in the shape of a cross with shops on the main street and administrative buildings on the cross street. Snaking out from the sides were several dirt roads that picturesquely wound their way out to numerous farms and small houses. This appeared to be where the bulk of the people of Ulthar lived—if you judged by the people coming and going.

In the center of it all, there was an actual town square. This was where Foolishness led us. Almost every building had some sort of cat motif adorning it in the form of statues, metal silhouettes, and etched glass. People watched the cat lead us toward a door with a sign emblazoned above it: *Einar's Place.*

The cats watched us as well. There were dozens upon dozens of cats in the streets, on porches, in windows, and in the alleys between buildings. All of them looked healthy, well fed, and clean. Several smaller ones, older than kittens but not quite adults, followed us. There were no meows, hisses, yowls, or trills normally associated with cats. Just the soft murmur of voices from humans and felines alike.

Rather than being strange, this felt appropriate. As if it were meant to be. I gave the village and our watchers one last look before I entered Einar's Place after our escort and my patient. Inside, I found myself in a tavern, clean smelling and welcoming. Long tables lined the almost empty room. Two people and three cats turned as we came in.

I froze. One of the people looked like Malachi. Just as I was about to call out to him, he laughed and stood. I was mistaken. That wasn't Malachi. He was too different in stature and tone. I just wanted him to be my dead patient, well again. The man looked over his shoulder, a smile playing about his lips as if he knew he'd fooled me.

Josephine touched my shoulder. "We need to wait."

"Yes." I nodded. I looked from her to the man and found him gone. I shivered, unsettled. "All right."

Foolishness wound himself through our ankles. "I'll find Insightful." The cat disappeared among the legs of the tables and chairs.

Josephine chose a table and sat. "I remember when my brother first brought me here."

"Your brother?" I furrowed my brow. Ah, yes. Leland.

"Sometimes, we would meet in dreams. When he thought I was old enough, he brought me here." She gave me that sly smile of hers. "Our parents did not know. They had a time line for everything. Sometimes, we skipped the time line."

"I don't have a brother or any siblings. What was it like?"

Josephine smiled to herself. "It was terrible and lovely at the same time. Leland was older than me. Sometimes, I think he resented me as the youngest. We fought over so many things. But he was my big brother and he protected me from all who would do me harm."

I glanced at the ceiling with its large, dark wood beams. Leland might be the source of her grief, but I could not remember how he had died. Just that he had passed. "It sounds like a complicated relationship."

"It was. The older I became, the more we understood each other." Her smile disappeared. "Then he left, as all siblings must do in the end." She hugged herself and turned away, ending the conversation.

I sat across from Josephine, watching her and letting the silence grow until she relaxed into that familiar waiting pose. The tavern was like the rest of the village: it looked like a tavern you would see in picture books. The artwork wasn't exactly normal pub fare, however. A framed silhouette of a cat, gold against a black background, hung above the hearth. I gestured to it. "They really like their cats here."

"Of course we do." A heavyset man approached with a couple of tankards. "They're the eyes and ears of the god Ulthar." He gave me a curious look at my obvious lack of knowledge. "Real kitten here, eh, Josephine? Where'd you dig her up?"

Josephine folded her hands. "Good day, Einar. Please meet Dr. Carolyn Fern. She is my doctor and a good one at that." Although her tone of voice was smooth and polite, her mild rebuke was plain.

"Pardon, uh, Doctor." Einar put the tankards on the table. "Didn't mean any disrespect. It's just strange here in Ulthar for someone to not know of Ulthar." He glanced at Josephine who nodded her approval. "Ulthar was put on earth to watch the other Elder and Outer Gods. It's said that if things go too wrong, Ulthar will reveal himself and deal with them."

I glanced between Josephine and Einar. "Elder Gods?"

He shook his head. "We don't say their names. Not even here where we're so blessed and protected."

Josephine nodded. "So true. I will explain them later."

"*I* will explain them sooner." This came from a small, long-haired calico cat not much bigger than a loaf of bread. She leapt to the table and sat, wrapping her tail about her paws.

Einar looked uncomfortable. "Anything for you, Insightful?"

The cat shook her head. "No. I have business with these two."

Fascinated, I watched as the cat commanded the room. Her presence was enormous despite her small body. Einar ducked his head and hurried away. Josephine and Foolishness both regarded Insightful with respect.

"Welcome home, Josephine. Welcome, Carolyn."

"Hello."

Sometimes when Insightful spoke, it looked like she actually spoke in words. Sometimes, it looked like she spoke with only her body. "You don't have much time and you have much to do while you are here." Insightful twitched the end of her tail. "But, it's dangerous for you to be so naïve to the true ways of the universe."

"You speak of these otherworldly gods?" Just saying those words gave me a shiver. It reminded me of the spiral I'd started to fall into while looking at the marks on Josephine's back. "Who are they?"

"Your world is but one facet of many."

The cat inclined her head toward a ring on the table I hadn't noticed before. I picked it up, shocked at its familiarity. "This is my mother's."

"And will be yours when she passes. I know. I plucked it from your mind. Look at the emerald. The top facet is the world you know, Earth. Do you see the facets to the sides? This one is the Dreamlands. That one is R'lyeh. Each of the others is a different plane of existence, but part of the whole."

As the cat spoke, I found myself not only holding the ring, but standing on top of the emerald itself. I watched the tiny version of me upon the precious jewel. Around me, the tavern persisted, yet became even more unreal.

"Look within the gem. Do you see the other facets? The Elder Gods live here, the Outer Gods there. They want to be on the top."

Both versions of me watched the play of light through the gemstone. "The facets are moving."

"Yes." Insightful walked at my side even as she sat on the table before me. "The facets move. When the edges of the other planes come into contact, beings of that plane can cross over. When all the edges come together…"

"When the stars aligned…" Josephine walked on my other side.

"The gods travel. When that happens, the order is upset. We, the cats of Ulthar, watch and wait and try to prevent that from happening. We don't always succeed."

"What happens when you fail?"

"Madness and death."

All at once I was singular again, sitting in the tavern with Josephine and the cat. Insightful lifted her paw and pulled my mother's ring from my hand with a delicate claw. The ring disappeared as she did so. I sat back and pet the black cat that had snuggled into my lap, purring. I don't know when she arrived, but I was grateful for her warmth.

I gazed at Insightful's green eyes, the color of my mother's emerald ring. "I…"

"Ask your questions, Carolyn."

"What are these Elder…Outer…Gods?"

"Beings of great power. Ancient and alien." The cat shook her head. "That is not your question."

I flicked a glance at Josephine. She gazed at her clasped hands. "What does any of this have to do with my…with Josephine? I must help her. These nightmares. The wounds on her back." Josephine raised her head as I spoke her name, but she didn't say anything.

"That is the appropriate question." Insightful flicked her ears about as if listening to something. "The short answer is: everything."

"That isn't helpful." I tried to keep the irritation out of my voice. I failed.

The cat continued on as if I hadn't spoken. "The longer answer is this: your journey here is what will help or hinder Josephine. She has a duty. One she's forgotten—for good or ill. You also have a duty. To her. Thus her burdens are yours. Both of you will lose something important as soon as you gain what you need from this place. It's not an easy path you must walk. You have already met the one who will help you."

I shook my head. "I don't understand. You didn't answer my question. What do these gods have to do with Josephine's malady?"

"The edges of the planes also meet in a point. A point in time and space. A gate. A portal. These points are rare and dangerous. They have so much power. They are protected in the only way we know how." Insightful turned her attention to Josephine. "You've been gone for too long. You need to return to your childhood. You must remember what you already know."

Josephine pressed her lips together for a moment. "I think I remember the way."

The cat licked her paw then rubbed her cheek. "How you get there is of no consequence, as long as you get there." She turned back to me. "You will help her. In your duty, you will lose something so precious it makes me weep at the thought. But you will gain what you need—what you must have—to continue your own journey. This dream is merely the beginning."

None of this made sense. Not to my logical mind. But there was more here. I could feel it. Dream logic wasn't the same as waking logic. I pushed my frustration away. "Thank you for your... insight." Josephine smiled at me. My returned smile was quick and perfunctory. As interesting and unnerving as the idea of alien gods breaking into my world was, it was still just an idea. Surely they couldn't be actual *gods*.

I shook my discomfort off and pet the cat in my lap again. My patient was before me. She was very real, and she'd said something I could follow up on. I just needed time and privacy with her. "Josephine, I think it's time for us to go."

The black cat in my lap jumped down. I missed her warmth and comfort, but it was time to get to work. The cat rubbed against Josephine's ankle before she looked back at me. In my mind, I heard her say, *"In times of need, think of me."*

In a rush, I realized that the cat's name was Comfort and she was the reason I'd been taking these most outlandish revelations so well. It was a strange comfort to know that a talking cat kept me from going a little mad. Then again, I understood in all of this there was a journey I needed to take in order to help Josephine. I was willing to do so, no matter how odd or unbelievable.

Josephine and I left the tavern. I realized that neither of us had drunk from the tankards nor paid for the drinks. I wondered if, like in the fairy tales, one should not drink or eat in the Dreamlands. In truth, I wasn't hungry or thirsty, but we'd only just begun.

"Do you know where we're going?" I watched Josephine as much as I watched the beautiful buildings of the village that we passed by. Foolishness continued to escort us even as he took a moment to chase a flock of tiny flying books that scattered like butterflies at his half-hearted swipe.

Josephine frowned. "I...believe so. Insightful said 'back to my childhood' but I believe she actually meant to...to..." She stopped. "The idea is right there. I cannot reach it. There a veil between my grasping mind and the idea of it."

"Perhaps, Insightful meant a place you loved as a child?"

Her head came up. "Perhaps."

I could tell that she wanted to say more, although not here, not in such an open place. As we reached the edge of town, I halted and hunkered next to Foolishness. "Thank you for your help."

"My pleasure. Nice to get away from my duty every once and a while." Foolishness bumped his head against my leg.

I obliged him with a scritch behind the ears. "Do you have any other advice for us?"

"Yes. When you've done what you need to do, return *here*. If not to Ulthar itself, return to the glade where we met. I'm sure we'll meet again."

"Will we need to save you again?"

Foolishness flicked his tail back and forth. "Perhaps. Perhaps I'll do the saving. Just make sure you come back to this place. Don't try to leave through another path."

Josephine stroked his back. "We will."

I stood and looked toward the steep, rocky path we were to traverse. "Our path is before us. One step at a time." I led the way, wanting to put Ulthar and the talking cats behind me. More to the point, I wanted to speak with Josephine about what she wasn't willing to say in front of the cat.

Chapter 7

One of the hardest parts about being in the Dreamlands with Josephine was remembering that I was in a session with her and keeping that in the forefront of my mind. I was so very curious about where we were. I could not resist asking questions. The more I understood about the Dreamlands, the better I believed I would understand Josephine's control over it and herself.

With the dirt crunching beneath our feet and a breeze chilling the air, I began with something trivial. "Is it safe to eat and drink in the Dreamlands? I noticed you didn't drink what we were served."

Josephine shrugged, her breath coming in soft pants. "It depends. Ulthar is a safe place."

Her response sounded like a ritual phrase. I slowed my pace. I was used to fast walking between patients and buildings and errands. Josephine was not. When she caught her breath, I glanced behind to make sure we weren't followed. "You were saying something about a place you loved as a child?"

She nodded, walking with slower steps. "I mentioned that I have always been a vivid dreamer. Almost everyone in my family is. We are taught at a young age how to shape our dreams.

To combat the nightmares."

This was not what I expected from such a genteel and well-regarded family. It seemed they did more than encourage the fantasy. "You, your brother, your parents, all learned to lucid dream?"

Josephine considered this. "Lucid dream. That is an appropriate term."

"Frederik van Eeden, a Dutch psychiatrist, created the phrase in 1913. I read it in one of his papers. I attempt to practice this from time to time." I glanced at her. "I've been successful here, in this session with you."

"We *are* in the Dreamlands." Josephine spoke with the air of someone stating something obvious. "When I dream I almost always come here. But not lately. Not since I began having the nightmares. Not that I remember. Perhaps that is my problem. I have forgotten so much about dreaming and the Dreamlands. I don't understand how that could happen."

There was something I was missing. Something important. We were not truly dreaming. Were we? We were in a hypnotic session in my office. This, all this, around us was not real. The fact that Josephine accepted it without question was disturbing. What if I couldn't pull her from her fantasy? "Where do you believe you've been going if not here?"

"My mind. Only within my mind."

"What's within your mind that frightens you?" I wanted to pull the conversation toward the concept of grief and the dead Thomas Ruggles, but Josephine ignored my question to continue her narrative.

"From a young age, I always had friends here within the Dreamlands. Your patient, Malachi, he was one of them. We would meet at the Red House. He felt safest there." Josephine lowered her voice. "He was afraid of the Darkness that Watches." She raised her voice again to a normal level. "It couldn't see him in the Red House."

As before, my tongue was struck dumb. Those were the words Malachi had used to express his fear before he was murdered. She *had* known him. There was no other explanation. How an itinerant man knew—was friends with—a young woman like Josephine Ruggles could only happen in dreams. I did not want to consider the implications.

Yet, I had to. Josephine knew Malachi. Malachi suffered from nightmares and delusions—delusions that had somehow murdered him with a physical knife. How could dreams manifest in the real world? The answer was before me in the form of my patient. Through the mind. Her dreams were made manifest in her flesh in the form of glyph-like wounds.

Yet the mind couldn't bring a rune-covered knife from dreams into reality. Nor leave it behind in a cooling body. That was impossible.

"This is the place I believe we need to go. It was where I remember being when I was last in the Dreamlands. It is a hidden place. A safe haven. Many of my friends from here meet there."

Josephine had her back to me now. She'd pulled ahead, unaware of my distracted state. I forced myself to focus on her. "How far away is it?"

She paused and looked around. We were high in the mountains now. "I...I don't know. Only some of this is familiar to me."

Josephine stood there, her head turning to and fro as if to get her bearings. I didn't understand. There was only one path. As I watched her, something bulged out of her back. It looked like a book pressed against the fabric of her shirt. I stumbled and went to one knee. The pain of striking the hard rock surprised me. When I looked up again, Josephine waited, her head tilted at a quizzical angle. "Your back." It was all I could say.

I pulled myself to my feet as she craned around, trying to see what I saw. I hadn't torn my pant or broken the skin. My knee ached. That, in and of itself, upset me. But the blood on Josephine's back, upset me more.

"What is it? What's happened?" Her voice was high with panic and fear. She turned around and around, trying to see what I saw.

I grasped her by the shoulders. "Wait," I commanded as I shifted to look at the blood. It was on the lower left side of her back where the corner of the book had pressed out of her flesh. I touched it. Dried blood on the fabric scraped against my fingertip. "Does this hurt?"

She shook her head. "No. What's wrong?"

I pushed harder. "Now?"

"No. Please, Doctor, is there something wrong?"

"You have a bit of blood on your shirt where my fingers are."

I hesitated. Should I tell her the rest? Yes. I needed to. "There was the impression of something rectangular pushing out of your back against your shirt. It startled me. Did you feel anything?" I shifted to watch her face even as she turned to hide it from me. "Josephine?"

"There is no pain."

"But?" There was more. So much more. I needed her to tell me.

"I felt something within. It *wants* out."

I squeezed her hand, trying to encourage her. "Do you know what it is?"

She shook her head. "No. But I know who would know."

"Who is that?"

Josephine gazed ahead. "We need to go. I think I hear the Black Wind." She headed up the stone path.

I had no choice but to follow. Every conversation with my patient brought more questions. For now, I would ignore the mention of this "Black Wind." It was a delaying tactic. I had to know what she was hiding within. Literally and figuratively, it seemed. I walked alongside her, our pace matching step for step. I was stronger than she was. I could outlast her. I had to. "You know two things you haven't told me. If you want my help, you must trust me to help you."

We walked on in silence for a good minute. It seemed much longer than that. The more we walked, the higher and colder it became. No longer in rocky hills, we were in the mountains. Though, the path was still clear.

"I was given something to keep safe. I remember that much. I cannot remember exactly what it was. I do know it is important to my friend. She gave it to me and made me promise to keep it safe." Josephine paused on the path, her brow furrowed in concentration. "I was not supposed to look at it. I think…I believe I did."

"Was it a book?"

Josephine blinked her dark eyes, peering into my face. "There are some things man is not meant to know. There are other things that man must be prepared for before they witness it. When your life is as mine is, you need all the protection you can get."

Josephine's true malady took shape. "You learned something you shouldn't have."

She nodded. "I believe I must return what my friend gave me."

"Return to her or give to another?"

"To her. It is my duty to protect it as it protects me." Josephine hugged herself, shivering because of something other than the cold.

"Protect you from what?"

Josephine shook her head. "I dare not say the name again."

Was it this Black Wind she'd mentioned before? Was it more than a distraction? I turned her toward the path again, trying to focus on what was important. "Tell me about your friend? The one who gave you the book?" It was a book. That much was certain. What knowledge it represented was still unknown.

"I…" Josephine's shuddering interrupted her words. With a visible effort, she regained some composure. "She is a child. She is a wise woman."

"I don't understand. She's a child and a wise woman? What's her name?"

"I don't remember. Why can't I remember?" Josephine stopped where she was and hunkered down, burying her face in her hands. Soft sobs escaped her attempt to hide them from me.

I hunkered next to her, going to one knee, rubbing her back. "There, there. It's fine. It's fine. You'll remember soon enough." That was when I realized her clothing had shifted from the adventure wear back into the blue linen dress and heavy silken dressing gown. Her admirable control had slipped away. This was the time to push, to get deep into her psyche. "You'll remember. You're afraid of remembering. Why are you afraid?"

Josephine shook her head, still covering her face.

"It's time to stop being a child, Josephine. You need to help me if I am to help you. Tell me what happened. Why are you afraid?"

"The book. I read from the book. I wasn't supposed to. It whispered to me in dreams. I wasn't supposed to read from it. I was supposed to protect it as it protected me!"

She gasped in pain and twisted. Under my hand, the form of a thick book pushed against the fabric of her clothing. I felt the edge of the book dig into my palm. Something whispered to me. I yanked my hand back as if scalded. Josephine surged to her feet and stumbled to the side of the mountain. She leaned against the rough rock, panting. "The book was not meant to be read. Not by me." She gave me a piercing glance. "Not by you."

I stood, uncurling slowly, at a loss for words. The book tried to force itself out of her. I felt it. I could not deny it. But what did that mean? Did it represent something that Josephine knew, something dangerous? Or was my mind playing tricks on me in this strange place?

Something hovered on the edge of my awareness. Something I did not want to examine. This world. The Dreamlands. They were a figment of Josephine's considerable imagination. Yet, I experienced it too.

Above us came an unearthly cry. I froze. A nightmarish creature assaulted my mind with its alien wrongness. Bulbous eyes protruded from its horse-shaped head and its cry revealed sharpened teeth. The sound of its leathery wings beat the air. It was huge. So huge; the largest creature I'd ever seen. Watching it come with its scales and serpentine tail, I could not look away. Even as I wanted to flee, I did not—could not—move. I watched it come at me with talons outstretched, yet I was rooted to the spot. How could such a monstrosity exist? It was like nothing I'd ever imagined, or even dreamed of in my worst nightmare. Part of me screamed to move. The other part stared at my oncoming death like a deer in a bright light. I closed my eyes.

Something slammed into me. A moment later, I opened my eyes and found myself on the ground, looking at Josephine. She'd pushed me out of the path of the creature's claws.

"Shantak! We must flee. They'll dash us against the rocks." She took my hand and pulled me up behind her.

We ran.

There was still only one path; a winding rocky road butted against the mountain on one side and a sheer drop off on the other. Behind us the shantak screamed and gave chase. Just as we were hemmed in by the mountain, they were thwarted by it as well.

There were two of them. They darted in from the left side and from behind. They couldn't get close enough to grab either of us. We had rocks to throw and the mountain to keep them at bay, but I didn't know how much longer these would ward them off.

I kept Josephine ahead of me. The danger had paradoxically given her the focus she needed to regain her composure. She was the expert in this realm—whether she remembered everything or not—and she was our best hope for escaping the monsters that pursued us.

In the distance, I could see a stone bridge spanning the chasm. Even though there was plenty of room to flee to the other side, I couldn't see how we'd get across harried by monsters that should not exist. Still, we fled. We had no other choice.

We rounded a sharp bend and hesitated. Not more than one hundred yards before us was the end of our path. Our choice was a rock wall to put our backs to, or the bridge that crossed the chasm. There were no other ways to flee.

Behind us, the shantak screamed again.

Chapter 8

I prefer to think about things before I do them. I plot, plan, and consider. I rehearse conversations in my head, research before I write, and decide my route before I travel. I dislike improvisation in uncontrolled circumstances. It is who I am and who I have always been.

However, there are times when I cannot be in control. When I act on instinct, I am usually correct. Usually. I believe appropriate, instinctive actions come from a lifetime of planning and experience. It is only after the fact that I understand what I did and why.

Josephine and I ran until we could go no farther without traversing the bridge I'd thought was stone. This close to it, I saw that it was not stone, but ice and wide enough that two cars could pass each other. My stomach roiled at the thought of crossing that chasm on an icy bridge.

"What do we do?" Josephine stood close at my back.

I looked around for handholds—up or down—for us to climb to safety. There was nothing. Worse, the sky above darkened and swirls of light that looked suspiciously like eyes appeared to watch. The wind picked up and the clouds began to roil as if alive. Lightning lit the clouds from within, followed by the crashing boom of thunder. There was no help there. Even the mountain itself had taken on a malevolent quality, looming over us. Our only escape from the shantak was the bridge of ice.

Then I remembered my father's pistol. It was already in my hand, waiting for me to realize it was there. I checked both the magazine and the chamber. I had six rounds to protect us. Steeling my resolve, I set my stance and took aim. "As soon as I start firing, you get across that bridge. I'll follow." I kept my fear to myself. If I appeared confident, Josephine would trust that I knew what I was doing.

"I am ready." Josephine lifted her robe to make sure she didn't tread on it as she fled.

"Good. Go." I fired my first shot at the closest shantak monster. My shot was true. I hit it in one of its bulbous eyes. My next shot struck it in the neck. Josephine sprinted away, across the icy bridge on nimble feet. I watched as the wounded monster crashed into the mountain and flailed its bat-like wings, keening in pain. The second shantak turned from me to its fallen companion. My hopes for a feral response died in vain.

Instead of attacking and savaging its wounded peer, it landed next to it and licked at the blood. Not to feast, but to clean, to help, to heal. I backed up as the first monster went still and the second gave a cry of rage before launching itself into the air with great flaps of its leathery wings.

I sprinted after Josephine, expecting her to be at the other end of the bridge. To my horror, she stood in the middle of it, staring down at the chasm beneath. "Josephine, run! Run!" The bridge that had seemed so reasonable moments before now seemed impossibly long and thin. My shoes couldn't gain purchase and I skittered across it in an unsteady gait.

As I reached Josephine, the creature above us screamed. Josephine shook her head, mumbling, "The minions of the Black Wind. How do they know I'm here? How can they?"

I aimed a shot at the shantak and fired—more to scare than to harm. "Josephine, go!"

She looked at me with fear-filled eyes. "They know I'm here."

I fired again, keeping the nightmare creature at bay. "We'll deal with it. Now go!"

A deep *crack* resounded through the chasm. It was the sound of breaking bone. It was the sound of the bridge we both stood on crackling beneath our feet. I looked down and realized that it *was* bone. The ice had been its flesh. At the same time, I reached out a hand and pushed Josephine toward the other side of the bridge.

As soon as my hand touched her, propelling her forward, my vision plummeted far below to the raging river I had not known was there. A boat filled with half-man beings seemed to reach up for me. They were men, but they had goat legs with cloven hooves and horns protruded from their heads. More demon than man, they shouted, "The Bride! The Bride is here!" Some with no faces gibbered and jeered in glee. Fear overwhelmed me as bile filled my throat.

Then they were gone and we were running across the bridge as it shattered beneath us. Josephine tumbled to her knees as we reached the other side. She disappeared in a shower of falling ice, bone, and stone, screaming.

Plunging my left hand down, I grasped for her. I *could* reach her. And I did. I found and gripped her wrist as hard as I could. She reached up and grabbed my arm with her other hand. I hauled her over the edge, back from the precipice. Josephine sobbed and clutched at me. For the briefest of moments, I hugged her tight. I wanted to fall into the relief of having caught her. I could not. In my other hand was my weapon. Above us, hell screamed its fury.

I aimed another shot, my fifth, and fired. It struck the shantak's tail, but didn't appear to slow it down. I surged to my feet and looked for shelter. Not twenty feet away was a door in the wall of the mountain. Framed in dark wood, and as neat as you please, it waited with the patience of a saint. I did not question it. The door looked as if it had been made for us. "There! Go there!"

There was no more time. The shantak was on me. It beat at me with wings of leather as its talons slashed the air. I dodged as best I could. It was not enough. One of its claws caught hold and pierced my shoulder, knocking me to the ground, pinning me there. I screamed my pain and beat at its leg, trying to free myself. My scrabbling hand couldn't get purchase on those slick, hard scales.

Fetid breath assaulted me as the shantak came in to bite. I pistol-whipped it to no avail. The shantak snapped at my face, inches from my nose. I did the only thing I could do. I thrust the pistol into its slavering mouth, pointed up, and pulled the trigger.

For a moment, it continued to flap its wings. Then it went slack and fell, its mouth ripping my father's pistol from my hand, as it hit the ground, half on and half off the cliff edge. Its talon tore at my shoulder as the monster's body slid over the edge of the stone. I thought I was going to go with it. Then strong arms wrapped themselves about my waist and pulled me back from the edge. The shantak's talons hung on, tearing flesh and cloth as I screamed. Then the talons, and the monster, were gone.

Pain-dazed and bleeding, all I could do was let those strong, tawny arms—Josephine's—pull me from the cliff edge, through the door in the mountain, and into darkness.

I leaned against a cool stone wall and put my hand to my left shoulder. Pain spiked and my hand came away wet. The sound of a match striking gave scant warning that light was coming. Then the vision of Josephine lighting a lamp came into view.

As did my blood-covered hand.

I was bleeding and in pain. You weren't supposed to feel pain in dreams. I'd never bled in a dream before. I tried to marshal my thoughts, my focus, my will to make the bleeding and the pain stop. Nothing happened. I was still wounded. Still bleeding.

This was real.

"We're in luck. This is a tunnel I know. A little red singing bird of Celephaïs lives here."

I ignored her. I stared at my bloody hand glistening in the lamp-light. I touched my torn shoulder again and gasped at the pain.

This *was* real.

This *was* happening.

This *world* was real.

The *Dreamlands* were real. I could die in this place. Josephine could die. I wasn't strong enough to save us both. Worse, I'd lost my father's pistol. No longer did I believe it still lived in my desk drawer. I'd lost my protection, my touchstone. I'd lost...

Malachi sprang to mind, one of our many conversations before a hypnotherapy session.

"You're still suffering from intense nightmares, or bad memories?"

"Well, Doctor, those are two things I've got a bit of trouble keeping straight."

"Malachi, let us see what we can do about that..."

He'd been telling the exact truth and I hadn't seen it for what it was. Those nightmares and bad memories had been one and the same. In my mind's eye, his hesitant smile morphed into the relaxed state of hypnotic sleep, then his brow furrowed with fear. I could hear him whispering.

"Shadow figures stood above me and blood dripped from their fingertips."

I hadn't believed him. I had been so wrong. The ones with curved knives had come for him. Even though he died with one of their knives in his heart, all I could remember were the glyphs drawn in his blood on the wall of his room.

When he told me the shadow figures had taken his last name— *"The Darkness that Watches"*—he'd told me the truth. They'd left one of their knives in his body and I still had not believed. I had been so blind. So arrogant and so blind.

A sound came to me. Someone kept saying the word "no" over and over.

That someone was me.

I couldn't stop myself.

"Shhh. Shhh." Josephine was by my side. "Listen to the singing. Listen. It's a bird of Celephaïs. Listen."

She put her fingertips to my lips.

I wanted to bite them.

The very idea of me biting my patient shocked me into stillness and silence. I listened. There was birdsong. It was sweet. It cascaded over me, relaxing my tense muscles. Pain receded. Although it did not disappear, it cleared my mind of its panic.

I wanted to fight the song's soothing touch, to lose myself to the panic, the fear, and to never have to think of what I'd just realized ever again.

"I need to look for something." Josephine's voice echoed in the tunnel. "I will be back. Listen to the singing. Listen to the bird."

My patient was trying to care for me. She was barely more than a child. I had a duty to her. I had to process what I now knew. For her sake as well as mine.

I leaned my head back with my eyes closed. Birdsong swelled. I fell into its ebb and flow. They say music soothes the savage beast.

In this case, it soothed the chaos of panic. I considered my position. Somehow—*Josephine did this*, my mind whispered, *she brought me here*—I was in this place called the Dreamlands. It was filled with monsters and allies. Somewhere in this land was a place Josephine called the Red House. It was a safe haven. There, Josephine would return something she was protecting and her nightmares would go away, thus, her madness. I would deal with the rest of her mental trauma back in the real world.

I bowed my head. I had been uncommonly deceitful—to Josephine and to myself. This whole time that I'd assured my patient I believed her, I had actually been waiting for the logical explanation to appear. I'd been waiting for Josephine to realize the lie she'd told herself to cover the pain of a trauma she did not want to face. Deep down, I had believed Dr. Mintz. I had believed that Josephine Ruggles was merely hysterical and was crying out for attention. That she had not actually needed help.

How many of my other patients in the asylum had I done such a disservice to?

Back in the asylum. Back on Earth.

I was not on Earth. I was in the Dreamlands. I was in another time and place. There was no denying it as blood leaked from my throbbing wounds, in time with my beating heart, to drip down my body and stain my clothes.

The more I accepted the fantastical idea that I was not on Earth, but in another time and space, the rest fell into place. I thought of the cats of Ulthar and of Foolishness. The orange cat had instructed us to return that way to leave. Thus, there was a way to go home. We were not stuck in the Dreamlands forever. Just long enough to do what needed to be done.

If I could be strong enough to accept what was happening.

I would.

I must.

I tried to straighten as the sound of Josephine returning obscured the birdsong. The pain was too great. This was a concrete problem I could deal with. I would have to have her bind my arm to my body. Looking up as my patient and the lamp returned, I was pleased to see she was again in her adventuring clothing. She, too, was fortifying her will once more.

Josephine knelt next to me and revealed a handful of small red feathers. "Feathers from the little red singing bird of Celephaïs. They heal wounds. As its song can heal the mind."

This would be the final proof. As if I needed more proof. I did, though. My rational mind did not want to believe in the irrationality of my situation. If the feathers healed me, I'd have no choice and could admit aloud I was in a different world with different rules that could be bent by an act of will. "What do I need to do? Eat them?"

She shook her head with a smile. "No. They are to be used like a poultice, although they work more quickly." Josephine eyed my torn shirt. "I am sorry. We will get you a new blouse from the trunk up ahead." She pulled a knife from a sheath at her waist and began cutting the shirt off my shoulders, revealing the bloody wounds.

"Where did you get that?" I nodded to the knife in her hand.

"The trunk. I remember now that we keep trunks of useful things in places we travel for just this sort of emergency. This is something my family started long ago. It was part of our training. This is not the trunk I created. Though, I have added to it over the years."

"I see." It almost made sense. I put my hand on my thigh, looking for and not finding the sheath to my father's pistol. The pang of its loss hit me again and I closed my eyes.

"This will hurt, but only briefly."

I opened my eyes and watched Josephine lay the small red feathers against my body where the shantak's talons pierced it. I gasped as the feathers stung like needles piercing my skin. Then, the pain disappeared as the feather melted into my flesh. Over and over, Josephine laid the small feathers against my wound to meld with my body. Each one took away more of the pain, closing the wound. As Josephine ran out of feathers, my wounds were fully healed. I noted that even the scratches on my right shoulder and collarbone had healed.

"Well then." I took a breath, let my worldview tilt upon its axis, and accepted it all. "The Dreamlands has some amazing aspects to it. When we return to our world, I'll have to write as much of it down as I can remember." Josephine helped me up. "We will remember what happens here, won't we?"

She looked at me, her dark eyes shining. "You understand. You believe. You finally believe."

I nodded. "I do now." I wondered if we were in two places at once or if, somehow, Josephine had brought our bodies through, too. I kept my questions to myself. One epiphany at a time.

She gave me a brief, fierce hug. "You were supposed to help me. To come with me. I knew it. You are my anchor."

I returned the hug out of duty and took pleasure in it. Josephine had failed on the bridge, but succeeded when I faltered in body, then in mind. I had not suspected she could, or would, do either until she acted. She walked a strange balancing act of weakness and fear while standing upon a core of willful strength. She was a complex woman. I had more to learn.

As a point, Josephine did not answer my question. That, in and of itself, was an answer. We probably wouldn't remember what happened here. Or, like a dream, would not remember for long. "Where is this trunk?"

"Of course. Of course. My doctor cannot traipse through the Dreamlands in a camisole and a torn blouse."

There was an airy joy in her voice I had not heard before. I wanted to question it. I wanted a shirt more. Goosebumps covered my exposed flesh.

The trunk was there at the opening of a cave. It had all the things you might need for an adventure—rope, light, canteens, clothing—as well as some more esoteric things—a doll, chalk, a mirror, rubber balls, and a mask. There was no food. Then again, I still wasn't hungry.

I chose a functional shirt that would keep me covered and somewhat protected. I was not surprised that it fit well; as if it were made for me. That was the way of things here. Things would work until they weren't supposed to work anymore. There was freedom in the acceptance of my new understanding of the universe—it was so much larger than I had imagined. My point of view had shifted to save my sanity. Already, I worked to incorporate the new knowledge into my worldview and my psychological tool chest.

Josephine snuffed the lamp. I gave her a quizzical look.

"We won't need it. I believe I know the way now. Someone else will need this in the future." She put the lamp in the trunk and shut it. The trunk locked itself with a *thunk*, the leather belts affixing themselves on their own. Rather than be horrified at the living trunk's action, I was charmed. It would protect its bounty from those who should not have access.

I turned my attention back to Josephine, replaying her words in my mind. I examined her face. Was that contraction from fear or a new level of comfort with me? Or, was it merely a contraction?

Josephine stood still with her hands clasped before her as she waited for my word to continue on. Her face held no answers. Not for the moment.

I gave her a professional smile tinted with concern. "Oh, it's good to leave it then. While you lead the way, we will speak of this Black Wind and his minions."

Her face fell. She cast her eyes to the ground.

I touched her shoulder to soften my words. "We're still in session. I'm still your doctor. We have things we must examine."

Josephine nodded, fear plain on her face. "If you wish."

Chapter 9

I remember the way Josephine said "doctor" to me at times in our journey. It was akin to the word "savior." I could not be that for her—as much as I wanted to be. I needed to be Josephine's guide, not her hero. This is always a dangerous time in the relationship between a patient and a doctor. The patient gives up all sense of responsibility and hands it, and their life, to the doctor. The power is as intoxicating as it is toxic. Nothing good can come of accepting such a responsibility. It was hard, though. I had grown fond of Josephine. Thus, I needed to coax her into confronting her great fear.

The cave was about the size of an amphitheatre with light emanating from an unknown source. Faint colors of blue, purple, and green swirled about us in slow eddies on the cavern walls and floor, making it hard for me to get my bearings. I refused to search out the source of the light and dismissed the impossible. The words "impossible" and "unlikely" no longer had meaning in this place. The rules were different. Logic wasn't king. Physics were an illusion. Dream monsters could hurt, even kill. I needed to be on guard for all of it.

Josephine led the way, picking her path across the cave floor, weaving her way through stalagmites adorned with jewels and half-covered by creeping moss. As I watched one stalagmite in particular, yellow-green moss surged over a garnet. A heartbeat later, the moss turned the deep red of the gemstone. A touch to one foot alerted me to a spot of creeping moss that had found me interesting. I pulled my foot away and hurried across the cavern to watch Josephine. Behind us, the room filled with the sound of creeping moss covering and consuming whatever it could.

Josephine paced before half a dozen openings in the cave wall. She paused in front of one tunnel and considered a couple of the others. The one before us was rough-hewn with tool marks of having been carved from the mountain. One of the other tunnels had wooden supports. A third had bricked walls.

"Where do these go? To different places?"

Josephine nodded. "There are many places in the Dreamlands. We want to stay in the west."

I refused to ask the question she wanted me to ask. I would not be distracted from our session. I needed to help her in the way I hadn't been able to help Malachi. "Toward the Red House?"

"Yes."

"Which one takes us there?"

Josephine looked between the three tunnels, her face a mask of confusion. "Things have changed."

I stood close behind her. "You can do this. You know this place. Go with your instinct."

"What if I get it wrong?" She leaned back to me.

I let her shoulder touch mine, taking comfort as much as giving it. "Then we will deal with it together. Choose. Time is of the essence."

Josephine glanced at me out of the corner of her eye as I cast her words at her. She pointed to the rough-hewn tunnel. "That one."

I stepped around her and into the tunnel. "Let's go." I gestured for her to walk alongside me.

Josephine hesitated then steeled herself. With a raised chin, she stepped to my side. We walked in. The tunnel, dim, was wide enough for three people to walk abreast. The light neither waxed nor waned. All around us, the rock of the mountain pressed in. I looked back. Darkness swallowed the entrance of the cavern. It was as if we traveled in a bubble of light. I counted fifty steps before casting my opening questions.

"Who is the Black Wind?"

Josephine took a breath. "One of the Outer Gods. He has another name. We do not speak it. If we do, he might hear. He is one of the gods who interacts with humans." She spoke like a child reciting a lesson.

"And his minions? Are they demons?" I suppressed a shudder at the memory of those men with horns and hooves.

"I do not know. They work for him. They hunt for him. I believe that is their purpose."

"They hunt you now?" Josephine nodded. Her hand sought mine and clasped it for comfort. I squeezed, encouraging her. "Why?"

"I…" Josephine shook her head. "I am special."

I waited for her to continue. She didn't.

We walked in silence, our steps eating ground. It felt as if we were walking a spiral even though the way was straight and narrow. I smelled the faintest breath of fresh air. The tunnel wasn't going to be as long as I thought it would be. "They called you the Bride." Josephine pulled away from me, walking faster. I let her go. I walked a couple steps behind, watching her stiff posture and fear. "Why?"

"I do not want to talk about that." She continued to march ahead. "I cannot. I have another duty. I must focus on it."

Her first duty, the protection of something within her that was killing her slowly. She was correct. We needed to focus on that for the moment. "Yes. You have a point. We can revisit the Black Wind another day. We will do so, soon," I promised, wondering if her fear strengthened her will enough to influence my mind. I shook my head. I could not, would not, think like that.

I shifted back to our previous conversations and the point we broke through. "Do you remember what it was you weren't supposed to know?"

"I read the book." Josephine's voice was a whisper almost lost to our fast steps.

The tunnel wound in a downward direction. "You were not supposed to read the book."

"No."

To Fight the Black Wind

There were two ways I could approach this. Only one of them dug into Josephine's motivations. "Why did you read it?" The light grew, tinted red. I could see the opening.

Shadows encroached around us, squeezing us until it was only possible to walk one behind the other. Even as the light brightened the end of the tunnel, promising a sweet relief, part of me would be forever left behind in the shadows that now clung to my arms, my hips, my legs. It was all I could do to keep myself from pushing Josephine forward, faster. But she had to emerge from the darkness on her own. Her confession would be both our salvations.

"I was afraid." Again, Josephine's voice was soft.

It was a weak admission. A red herring. "What were you afraid of? Why did you read the book?" Closer and closer the exit came. I didn't know what was waiting out there for us. I needed to know what she'd intended when she did what she'd been forbidden to do.

"I thought it would protect me." We crossed out of the tunnel and into the light. Josephine ahead with me at her heel. "I thought it would give me the spell to stop…" She hesitated, unwilling to go on in either word or step.

I stopped close behind, careful not to touch her. She had to take this final step on her own. Instead, I gazed at the beauty that lay before us.

It was a gorgeous valley with a forest at its center. Instead of verdant greens, the forest's leaves were the fall colors of browns, yellows, oranges, and—in the center—red. The path led down the hill and passed a babbling stream, winding into that forest. The sun above us shone bright at high noon. Josephine turned her face upward, letting the sun warm her skin. She had her eyes closed.

I lowered my voice and prompted her with her own words. "The spell to stop…?"

"My death at the hands of the Black Wind." Josephine whispered to the uncaring sky.

It seemed that the Black Wind needed to be spoken of sooner rather than later. How could this Black Wind kill her and why? What was within her that could stop something like an Outer God? "I don't understand."

The valley below us flickered. One moment it was lush mountainside, the next it was a roiling ocean with white capped waves.

I blinked and shook my head. The gorgeous flora returned.

Josephine turned to me. "I fear I have hastened my end. I read the book, and its madness brings the Black Wind ever closer. I should never have been so foolish. I must rid myself of this burden." She looked over her shoulder at the forest. "And I will. There, in the Red House." She took a step backward.

As she did, the landscape changed again. The valley disappeared and the angry ocean with its violent waves reappeared. Instead of flat ground, we were on slick rock. The wind howled around us. Josephine gasped, slipping and falling. I reached for her. Our fingertips touched and then she was gone, tumbling to the rocks.

Josephine hit the ground of the valley hard. She'd landed on the path that led us into the heart of the forest below. I hunkered, waiting for the land to change again. It did not. I stood and focused on thinking we were in the valley of the Red House, hoping it would keep us stable.

"Josephine?"

For a moment, she did nothing except lie there on her back. She screwed up her face in a way that made me think she was going to laugh. It would've broken the sudden darkness of the situation and deflected her fear and the uncertainty of our surroundings.

She didn't laugh.

Josephine arched with a shriek of pain and turned over. Her back bulged and moved under her shirt. She pulled her tucked blouse out of her pants and craned her neck. We both saw the book-shaped thing press against her skin, its corners cutting through, blood leaking through punctured flesh. Josephine gasped in pain. "Get it out. Help me, Doctor! Please!"

Falling to my knees, I pulled the ornate knife from the sheath at her belt, then pressed a hand to her shoulder. The book, a literal book, had to come out of her. "Still, Josephine. Lie still."

"It hurts. Please." Her words were a panic, but her writhing body stilled.

I pushed her blouse up, exposing her back. With a single slash, I cut her flesh from hip to hip. The book, impossibly large, poked out of that slit. I slid my hands under her skin and grasped the book by its sides. It was slick, like the scales of the shantak I'd fought. I refused to let go. Sliding one arm farther under Josephine's skin almost up to my elbow, I caught the corner of the book. I eased it downward and out from under her skin.

The book resisted, catching on something within my patient's body. She gasped in pain and clawed at the ground. "Please," I whispered. I don't know who or what I begged to help me, but providence heard and the book acquiesced. My hands found purchase and the book slid out of Josephine's body. At the last moment, it stuck and I yanked as hard as I could. The book released Josephine with an audible pop that she echoed with a moan of relief.

I rocked backward and hit the ground with a hard thump. The book—that had seemed so big—pressed against my body, the size of a bible but only half as thick. I pulled it away from me, expecting to be covered in blood, but the book and my shirt were clean.

She still lay on the ground, panting, laughing, crying. Her back was unmarked and unmarred from what had just happened. Even though I'd cut her and the knife I'd used lay discarded at her side, her tawny-beige skin was smooth. I couldn't believe it. "Are you well?"

Josephine pushed herself to her knees and brushed the dirt from her clothes in an absent gesture. She twisted around and looked at her back, touching the unblemished skin. Her smile was beatific as she gave another sigh. "I am free. You have freed me."

I looked down at the book in my arms. Its blank cover now revealed a title in that script that was both so familiar and alien. I could almost understand it. Almost.

She touched my shoulder and offered me a hand up. "I knew I needed you on my journey. Thank you for having the strength I did not."

I accepted the hand and the compliment as gracefully as I could. While Josephine seemed much more balanced, I felt off kilter. As if I stood on an unseen boat. "Now that I've done this, we need to get the book back to its rightful owner." Josephine did not ask for the book—her duty, her responsibility, her burden—and I did not offer it.

Josephine pointed down the path toward the colorful woods. "Perhaps…perhaps this has pushed my doom farther away."

I breathed slow breaths. "As soon as we give this back to its owner, we will speak, you and I, of the Black Wind and why you believe it means your death."

I wanted to talk about the Black Wind, to continue our session, but I couldn't. Not while I held the book. My mind was too full. I glanced at the book's cover again. I could almost understand what it spelled out. In the back of my mind, the book whispered, tempting me to open and read it. To understand. To know. To become one with it. I now understood the real reason Josephine read the book.

I resisted its temptation with years of study instead of play, years of discipline instead of whim, years of refusing immediate gratification in order to gain my heart's future desire. Still, the book called to me even though I knew that path was madness.

I didn't know how long I could resist its whispered pleas. Here, in my hands, was true magic. I was curious. So very curious.

Chapter 10

There are moments when action becomes instinct and instinct becomes action. Without knowing how or why, you intuit what you need to do and you do it. There is neither thought to consequences nor thought to retribution. There is the obstacle and an epiphany regarding what needs to occur. It is only after the deed is done that you can reflect upon your actions and determine if they were correct or not. For me, these moments are rare. I both adore and loathe them.

Josephine walked with a light step ahead of me. I let her lead the way as I silently recited poems, quotes, and lectures to keep the whispers at bay. All the while, she chattered as if at a social tea. I listened as close as I could and responded when I could utter the appropriate words. There were only so many things I could do at once.

"This has always been one of my favorite places in the Dreamlands. Ever since I was a little girl. This is where I met Malachi and Luke and Mimi and Playful and so many others. The valley is safe. That is why it exists. The danger comes from traveling to or from it. That is when things happen. At the transitions."

Josephine's voice had taken on an earnest, childlike quality. As if she were regressing to childhood. I worried. Now, I carried her duty and burden because I needed to. Would I be able to get her to take responsibility for herself once more? There is a freedom in handing one's life over to another in authority. Especially after you have experienced the heaviness of duty and adulthood.

Especially one as heavy as the book I carried. I pulled it from me to look at the incomprehensible writing on its front again and was surprised that I could read it. *The Glyphs of the Eltdown Shards and the Binding Language.* There was no author listed. Just the title.

I was learning by osmosis. This realization kept me from opening the book to look for the name of the author. I'd never encountered a book that was dangerous to hold. Then again, I'd never traveled to another world before. It was strange how calm I felt now that I'd accepted the impossible.

Hugging the book once more, I looked to my surroundings. We'd entered the forest, its huge trees towering cathedral-like above us. Leaves crunched underfoot, but the dirt path was clear of debris. It wove its way through the trees toward a building in the distance.

"Is that the Red House?" My heart sped up and hope flooded through me. There was an end to the journey.

"Yes. Mimi should be there."

"Who's Mimi?"

Josephine paused, tilting her head. "Oh! Mimi is my friend. The one who gave me the book. She will know what to do now."

As one, we hurried our steps, all but running toward the house in the distance. Around one large tree, the path became a straight line and I could see why the building was called the Red House.

Sitting in the center of a small glade, the house had red walls and white trim around the doors, windows, and eaves. The roof was covered in slate grey tiles that reflected the red-tinted sunlight that shone down upon it through the trees. If the forest were a cathedral, this was its chancel. Was an altar within? Outside, sitting on the wide, white porch, was an old woman. She watched us come without a sound. Only the rocking of her chair told me she was alive.

Josephine ran ahead. "Mimi! Mimi! I made it back."

I slowed my steps to watch Mimi and Josephine meet, not wanting to interrupt. Their voices carried as if I were next to them.

Mimi stood and embraced Josephine. "So you did." She held Josephine at arm's length. "You've grown, girl. But not as much as I had expected."

Josephine touched Mimi's greying hair. "What happened? Why…why are you so old?"

"It's been years…decades…for me here. I've been waiting. Time passes differently in the Dreamlands. You should remember that."

My heart and my feet stuttered to a stop. This was something I hadn't known or considered. How much time had passed back in my world? Josephine's next words soothed my worry.

"But, it's only been a couple of weeks. How could it have been so long for you?"

Mimi turned from Josephine to look at me. "You've brought me a guest."

Although her voice was neutral, I recognized the disapproval in it. I wasn't sure why it was there, but I needed to take command of the situation to make sure the book was returned to its rightful owner. I strode up to the porch. "Hello. I am Dr. Carolyn Fern. Josephine is my patient. We've come to return something to you."

Mimi stepped down the stairs on unsteady legs. She shuffled over to meet me. Something about her was familiar. As if I had met her before. Perhaps long ago in another dream. She stopped before me and bowed her head.

"I remember you. You didn't listen to me. Why didn't you listen to me? I couldn't save her. I thought I could save you. Now all of us will live and die together. Our fates are intertwined." Her voice was tired and old and damnably familiar.

"I do not understand."

"Must you do this to me? Must you make me rip the scales from your eyes?" She tilted her head up, one golden-brown eye visible through her mass of greying-black hair.

Suddenly, I was back in the asylum, standing before Nurse Heather and Dr. Mintz's drugged patient. "Sati Das? How are you here?" I blinked, the image of the patient melded into the old woman before me, transforming her into a young Indian woman with a straight back, bright eyes, and long dark hair. That appeared to be her true form, her true age, despite the years I felt upon her shoulders.

"Mimi?" Josephine stood next to us. This Josephine was no more than ten years old. "What's happening?"

Sati took a breath and let it out in rush. "I'm sorry, Josie. I'm not in a mood to play." With that, she turned on her heel and strode into the Red House. She closed the door behind her.

"Doctor? What's happening? What's going on?" Josephine took my hand in hers.

I looked down. She was an adorable child. It would be so easy to allow her remain so. One more step to taking care of her and protecting that aura of innocence I knew was a lie. After all, I held the very book whose whispers she'd succumbed to. But she knew Sati, the woman she named Mimi, better than I did. I would need her insight, if not her support, to convince Sati to take back the book that clamored for my attention. "I'm not sure. But I think you need to grow up again. I may need your help in there."

Josephine shook her head. "I don't wanna."

"There are many things I don't want to do. So, unless you want this book back…?" I held it out to her. She let go of my hand and stepped away. "I thought not. Grow up and come help me with this." I refused to believe she would deny me.

I raised my chin and faced the Red House. It was going to let me in if I had to tear it down piece by piece. I strode to the front door and tried the doorknob. It turned in my hand without hesitation. I went in, leaving Josephine behind.

All the while, *The Glyphs of the Eltdown Shards and the Binding Language* wordlessly shouted in my head for me to read it.

I walked into a single room with four doors leading off of it. All of the doors were closed. This was a parlor where you could invite people into the house, but not necessarily into the home. Three overstuffed chairs and a long couch sat in a horseshoe around a long, low table on bird legs in front of a fireplace. All of it was decorated in rich hues of reds, oranges, and yellows. The occasional adornment in blue broke up the fierce color pattern.

Sati, once more the old woman I saw on the porch, stood next to the fireplace with a straight back and grey hair in a neat bun. She gazed into the fire's flickering flames. Rather than wearing the sari of her native land, she wore the business dress and jacket of a professor. In my mind's eye, the memory of her true form, the drugged woman in the asylum, flickered in and out of existence.

"We are not done, you and I." I moved into the room and took a seat in one of the overstuffed chairs. "This book. It belongs to you."

"And if I refuse to take it?"

"It's killing Josephine." I didn't say that it was currently gnawing on my will in an effort to get into me.

Sati turned. "It appears that Josephine is no longer in danger." She gestured.

I looked and saw Josephine standing by the porch door. She was once more a young woman, but she was also back in her linen dress and dressing gown. I knew what it meant. Sati did not. "Josephine is still in danger. You gave her a duty too much for her. I know exactly what she went through and why she succumbed."

"I *am* standing here in the room with you both. Do not speak of me as if I were not." Josephine pulled her dressing gown about her in an effort to salvage her dignity.

Sati rolled her eyes. "Then come sit down and be part of the conversation."

"Perhaps I should throw this book into the fire." My statement was met with a fierce reaction from both Sati and Josephine.

"No!" Josephine, in the act of sitting, jerked to her feet again. "You cannot."

"No. We would lose too much." Sati took two steps toward me, revealing what she'd kept hidden thus far.

"I can take it back. I'm strong enough." Josephine reached a hand toward me. "I know better now. Don't throw it into the fire."

I ignored Josephine's hasty, panicked words. I only had eyes for the scroll case in Sati's hands. About a foot long and two inches in diameter, the beige leather was covered in embossed swirls and whirls accented in gold. It was beautiful. It was important. I recognized it in the depths of my soul. It was what I'd been meant to carry all along.

"I see..." I breathed these words, putting my understanding of Sati's burden and the reason she didn't want the book back into the breath, and locked eyes with the professor.

Sati shook her head. "I've already ripped one set of scales from your eyes. Don't make me rip another."

"There is little more you can do to me that has not already been done. Those horses have escaped the barn." It was true. There was no going back to the way I once was. "All experiences shape us."

"It will change more than just you." Sati raised her eyes to Josephine.

"It must be done. You must take this back." I raised the book to her despite the pain I felt at parting it from my body. Sati remained where she was. I put the book on the table between us. "I will take on your burden."

Sati raised the scroll case then lowered it again as she shook her head. "I…" She fell silent.

I was missing something. I focused on the professor. There was guilt and fear in her posture. She'd turned away from Josephine. "Why did you give Josephine the book? Why would you give something so dangerous to a child?"

"It wasn't supposed to hurt her." Sati's eyes begged for forgiveness. "It wasn't awake when I held it."

"What changed?"

Sati shook her head. "I don't know. It never occurred to me that she would read it. It was a barrier, a ward. Something to hide behind. It wasn't awake. I didn't know it *could* wake."

I could feel the book thrumming on the table. It seduced me with its promise of knowledge and power. "It is awake now."

Josephine moved between us and reached for the Eltdown Shards book. Her body froze scant inches from it. As she froze, so did we all. Three women in a tableau of need and conflict. I reached for Josephine with one hand and for the scroll case with the other. Sati held the scroll case with both hands, already pressing it toward me. Our conversation whirled about the room in visible thought bubbles as if we were nothing more than characters on a page.

"I am right here! Neither of you is listening to me. This was my burden. I should never have given it up." Filled with determination, Josephine strained toward the book.

Regret tinted Sati's words. *"It was my burden, but I could not handle two duties at once. I was weak. I thought I was doing the right thing."*

"I will take the Elder Sign from you. You will take back the book. Josephine will heal in heart and mind. It will change all of us."

To Fight the Black Wind

It was the only logical thing to do. I pressed my intent toward them, willing them to see things my way.

"Who am I if I do not have a burden to bear?" Josephine relaxed, but did not withdraw. *"My family are ever dreamers. They have been linked to the Dreamlands for generations. This is what we are meant to do."*

Sati's thought lashed across the tableau, making the room ripple. *"But at what cost, O Bride of the Black Wind?"*

Josephine did not answer. The tears that streamed down her frozen face were enough.

I focused on Sati, cutting Josephine out of the conversation. *"Professor Das, I know you were in a coma. It must have had something to do with the Eltdown Shards."* I ignored the book as it writhed against me. I didn't know when I had picked it up again. *"This book is your burden. The Elder Sign must be mine. I will do what needs to be done."*

Sati's image brightened at the use of her title. *"If you do this, your relationship with Josephine may be torn asunder. Is this a risk you are willing to accept? Do you take the Elder Sign knowing you may lose your patient forever?"*

Part of me struggled with this conflict. My patient came first. More than that, Josephine was a wonderful young woman who had much to give the world. If I took the scroll, I could damage Josephine. But, if I didn't ensure that the book went back to Sati, I would lose Josephine to the nightmares once more. It was a choice between could and would. *"Yes. I will take that risk."*

The world shattered and fell about us. When all resettled once more, the three of us sat about the low table—Josephine in a chair with her hands folded, me in a chair holding the scroll case, and Sati, still in her old woman form, on the couch clasping *The Glyphs of the Eltdown Shards and the Binding Language* to her breast.

Josephine looked at each of us in turn, her face the smooth neutral of a well-bred woman with emotions to hide. "Well, it appears that is that. There is nothing more to do except go home."

"There is one more thing." I put the scroll case, now no bigger than my hand, in a pocket. "Tell me about the Black Wind." I allowed no argument in my tone of voice. She had evaded the subject long enough.

Chapter 11

As a Doctor of Psychology, I must be able to determine the differ-ence between an evasion, a false confession, and an admission. As every patient is different, coaxing and guiding them to reveal their great trauma is a delicate act of cajoling and supporting, con-vincing the patient to let go of what they fear most. Once they do this, they are shattered in a way that they can pick up their own pieces, with expert psychological assistance, until they are whole once more.

Josephine rocked back as if struck. "No. It's not safe to speak his name."

Even as she tried to refuse, I knew she would do as I demanded. "This is a safe place." I glanced at Sati for confirmation. She nod-ded. "You told me so yourself. It's only in the transitions that things happen. You have avoided this long enough. Tell me." I locked eyes with her and refused to let go.

My patient stared at me for a long time before her face changed—a hardness and determination I had not seen before coming to the forefront. "If you insist." She gathered her thoughts as she refolded her hands in her lap. "My family has always dreamed. We've always come to the Dreamlands. Even before the pact with the Black Wind. As soon as we start dreaming, our families mentor us to shape, to create here."

She unfolded one hand and held it up. Before our eyes, a bird came into being. Josephine set it aloft. The wren fluttered about the room until she gestured to the window. The wood and glass disappeared, allowing the wren to escape. With another gesture, the window reappeared. "All that we have learned has been in an effort to run, hide, and escape from the Black Wind."

"Why?"

"The pact. My many-times-removed grandfather, Elijah, bargained with the Black Wind. For what, I do not know. The end result is that one of every generation is marked by the Black Wind. What for? Again, I do not know. I am neither engaged to be married nor twenty-one. That is when all of this is explained. I only know as much as I do because of my brother, Leland. He came to me in his dying dream to warn me. He told me about my doom, then he died, leaving me to fend for myself."

Sati and I exchanged a glance. "Dying dream?" I asked.

Josephine pulled herself from the past. "Leland died almost six years ago in the Great War. As he lay dying on the battlefield, he chose to dream his life away. In that dream, he warned me that the Black Wind would mark me. That I was the only one of this generation left. I would be marked until I had children or I died in the Dreamlands."

"Then why are you called the 'Bride of the Black Wind'?"

She gave me a bitter smile. "I met him. First, at one of father's parties. Then, in my dream that night. A tall Egyptian man with a regal bearing and a piercing gaze. At the party, he was introduced as Rafiq Talhouni, a visiting antiquarian who specialized in books. In my dreams, as he marked me, he revealed his true name..." Josephine shuddered, forcing the name through her unwilling lips. "...Nyarlathotep."

As Josephine spoke, buttons appeared on her blouse. She raised trembling hands to unbutton them, revealing the smooth skin of her collar bones and breast. "I can hide the mark. But there are always those who can see it." Swirling gold marks appeared, covering her upper chest. They writhed upon her skin as if alive. Several of the tentacles shifted to reveal a single malevolent eye.

One that looked about with interest.

One that focused on me.

It could see me, see into my soul, measuring me for God knows what. I felt a tickle in the back of my head. It was the same feeling I had when the Eltdown Shards book begged me to let it in. I shivered in the chill of it, every hair on my body standing on end. It was more than I could bear. I turned away, shaking.

It could still see me, searing into my soul. It picked through my fears, examining them like a woman considering fruit; scenting them, feeling them, cracking them open wide. All the while, I could do nothing to stop the invasion into my uglier imaginings and baser thoughts. I wanted to scream, but I couldn't catch my breath.

"Josephine, that is enough." Sati's voice was a smooth whip crack through the tension. "This place is safe, but inviting the likes of the Black Wind *in* would not be good for anyone."

Josephine did not respond in words.

The invasion within my mind ceased all at once. It left me stunned and trembling. I reached for my salvation—my work, my patient, my desire to cure Josephine.

I took several shaky breaths and forced my mind to push aside the horror of what had just happened. I faced the problem head on, trying to find an answer to help her. "You are the Bride because you're marked. You don't know everything, but according to your brother, you are the chosen one until you have children—who presumably will then become chosen—or die in the Dreamlands." I raised my head and risked a glance at Josephine. "What does the Black Wind get out of you dying?"

Josephine was properly covered once more with her hands folded in her lap. "I do not know. I believe the book protected me as much as I protected it. I...do not know what to do now. The book *anchored* me."

She spoke as if I should understand what she meant by the word *anchor*. I didn't understand. I glanced at Sati again. She shook her head. I wasn't sure if she indicated she didn't know or she couldn't tell me. "I believe, now that the book is back with its rightful guardian, we need to journey home. The asylum is not safe for one such as you. Not with Dr. Mintz's interest."

Josephine frowned. "But, I should be well now. No more bleeding

84

nightmares. I can finally go home."

I nodded. "Yes. I can visit you at your home to continue our talks. I suspect it will be needed. No one is cured in one session. Mental trauma will not disappear simply because we have removed the source of the physical trauma."

The heiress bowed her head. "What do I do now? I no longer guard the book. I need a purpose."

"That is something we can talk about in the real world."

Josephine's scowl marred her genteel face. "This world is as real as the next."

I made a calming gesture. "I misspoke. I apologize. I'm still learning. I meant we could speak about it outside the Dreamlands." I felt the need to return home as if it were a physical thing calling to me. The Dreamlands were too real, too alien, too dangerous.

"This is home to me."

"It is a home from time to time." Sati stood, ending what could have become an argument, with the motion. "Time is no longer on our side. The Black Wind is now interested in this place. I will not have it. I cannot fight him off. You both must leave. Now. The question is where will you go?"

She gestured to the front of the room where two doors stood. "The one on the right will lead you back to the Enchanted Forest. The other..." Sati closed her eyes and stretched forth a hand toward the door on the left. "The other is a path to the north...to the Plateau of Leng." She shook her head. "I don't know why that path appeared. It's both within the Dreamlands and outside it...in another space, another time."

Josephine stood and walked to the sinister door. "The Plateau of Leng. My family knows nothing of it. This could be my new path, my new duty. Investigate the Plateau of Leng." She smiled at me. "Just think of it, Doctor, we could discover something new. Something no one else knows of."

I stood, slow and reluctant. This was what I had wanted Josephine to do—take responsibility for her actions—but not here. Not in this world. Not in this way.

She said "we." She wanted me to go with her. Expected me to go, even. I needed to deny her without punishing her for taking the initiative. I could not journey to a place known as the Plateau of

Leng. I was barely holding on as it was.

"Such a thing could be exactly what you're meant to do, but I cannot go with you." I continued to speak even as her face fell. "I have other patients to attend to. Also, a job that requires my attention." I was too aware of the pain I caused her. I wanted to take it back. I could not. This was needed—for both of us. I walked over to the right door and examined it.

"But, I need you, Doctor. I can't…cannot…do it alone." Her voice was soft and pleading. It broke my heart.

I touched the warm wood, letting my fingers dance over the carving of the large tree. I didn't know if it was supposed to be the tree in the glade or not, but in my mind's eye it was. "You can, Josephine. You've spent your whole life visiting the Dreamlands on your own. You don't need me." I glanced at her. "I believe in you. You can take on this task, this journey, *alone*."

I didn't want her to. More than anything, I needed her to take my hand and to come with me. I wanted to be back in my familiar world—no matter how changed I was. The scales had fallen from my eyes. I would never be the same again. This had consequences I couldn't anticipate or consider right now.

I watched Josephine's profile as she faced the door she wanted to choose. "Or, perhaps you can begin your new task another day. After you've prepared for it. Come back with me." I offered her my hand.

She was afraid of being alone. She never was in her real life—I couldn't think of the Dreamlands as real. Not yet. Her face flickered with emotion: fear, longing, stubbornness, need. She turned to her door, touched the stone, and withdrew her hand with a start. "It is cold. Freezing." She rubbed her hands together.

I needed to make a decisive choice. I looked over my shoulder to say farewell to Sati Das. I wasn't surprised to see that she and her Red House were already gone. As was the valley. Once more, we stood on a rocky plain. There were *things* moving in the distance—moving toward us at inhuman speeds.

"Whichever path you choose, we must go now. I am returning to the Enchanted Wood to go home. Go to the Plateau of Leng or come with me. It's your choice, but you must make that choice now." I didn't wait for her response. To hesitate meant death. I threw a hand to her as I grabbed the doorknob and turned it.

"Please!" The door swung open, revealing the Enchanted Wood. As I stepped through, Josephine grasped my hand and held on for all she was worth.

I didn't have time to be relieved. The rocky landscape fell away, leaving us deep within the verdant forest that even I recognized. Behind us, the bandits with their horns and hooves jeered their hunting cries, coming ever closer.

Chapter 12

No doctor of the mind succeeds one hundred percent of the time. We all fail to help our patients. Some are just too far gone. Some are unwilling to leave their delusions behind. Sometimes, it is the doctor who cannot figure out the path needed to cure our patients of their maladies. It was there, in the Enchanted Wood, where I failed Josephine.

I still do not know what I could have done differently to save her.

Relieved more than I ever thought I would be, Josephine and I ran hand-in-hand, dodging branches and leaping over roots. The Enchanted Wood didn't seem as welcoming as it had before, but it didn't appear malevolent. Not yet. I focused on finding Foolishness. I had no idea where he was or what he could do against our pursuers—who seemed like both half a dozen and a horde of thousands.

Josephine pulled her hand from mine and I allowed it to happen. We could run better and faster side by side. "They're gaining."

They were. The minions of the Black Wind were only a few trees behind us. I had no weapon. My father's gun was lost to the chasm. Then I realized that I had no problems speaking or breathing. Had we been back on Earth, I would have been a broken wreck. "I know. Can't you do something? You've trained for this. Create weapons."

An explosion of sound erupted behind us and a metal spear stabbed itself deep into the tree next to Josephine. We hid behind another tree to look at the weapon. A long line of chain yanked it out of the wood. Josephine's face went neutral. Only the press of her lips into a white line showed her fear and determination. She raised both hands to the trees above her. Their fruit—large, green, bulbous things—pressed themselves to her. She flung these at our pursuers.

They flew unerringly as if birds on the wing and the sound they made upon impact, wet and sizzling, made me wince. Still, we both smiled as the bandits screamed their pain.

"That should make them a bit more hesitant." Josephine threw several more of the dangerous fruit then shook her hands as if they were hot.

"Yes." I gestured for us to go. We took off running. "We need to find Foolishness."

"In the Glade of the Haunted Moon Tree. It's where he's meant to be." Josephine leapt off of one protruding tree root up to a high branch. "Come, the branch roads will be faster." Without thinking about what I was doing, I mimicked Josephine's leap. The jump took my breath away. She steadied me as I landed. "We also have a better chance of finding a cat in the branches than on the ground where the zoog will attack him."

I laughed at the joy of being up so high. My laughter died at the first sound of gunfire and splintering of wood. Josephine and I took off running again. I dodged over and around branches that threatened to knock me from my height. I was equally cautious to avoid the glowing fungi and vines when they appeared in our path. Even in my haste, I saw that both were alive and hunting. Could these be used against our pursuers? "Why won't they climb the trees?"

"Two reasons. The first, cloven hooves are not meant to climb trees like these. The second, the trees do not like them."

I had no response. Both reasons made sense. A flash of orange ahead gave my heart hope that we would escape. "There!"

Josephine let out an unladylike whoop of joy and led me through the woven branch roads toward Foolishness. Behind, the bandits called and jeered in an incomprehensible language that hurt just to hear it. I shook my head and forced myself to go on. Josephine paused and faced our pursuers as I reached her. Again, she raised her fists high. This time, at her unspoken command, a wall of thorny vines sprung upward between us and the bandits. They wound themselves around the trees, linking them together in an armored lattice of living flora. The bandits howled their fury and pain as they rebounded off the barrier. The twining, writhing vines grew until they blocked the bandits from sight.

"I didn't know you could do that."

She looked at her hands. "Neither did I."

"The trees, the Enchanted Wood, helped." Said Foolishness. He sat on a branch in the distance. "Hurry. Hurry! We don't have much time. You have to get to the Haunted Moon Tree. That's your way out."

Josephine and I sprinted over and through the branches toward him. Leaves slapped at my face and my body. I did my best not to disturb them, but they seemed to leap into my way. Vines snaked out to trip me. Was the forest trying to delay me in order to save Josephine? I pushed the thought out of my head as the madness it surely must be. I ran harder through leaves that blinded me. I would survive. I would make it through.

Then I was falling.

I hit the ground with a hard thump and sprawled there, stunned. Behind me, sounds of pursuit rose as the barrier of thorns and vines fell. I pushed myself to my feet and looked around. We were in the glade where we first saved Foolishness. This time, the glade was huge. It would be like sprinting across the university.

Foolishness twined himself about my ankles. "You must climb the Haunted Moon Tree. It's the only way to escape now."

"Will it send us home?"

Gold-green eyes stared up at me. "Yes. It's your way out of the Dreamlands."

I stared at him, sensing there was more he was trying to tell me. The crack of gunfire as well as the explosion of the spear ballista told me I had no time to interrogate the cat further. "Josephine!"

She stood on the edge of the glade. "I can hold them back."

"No. It's time to go. We've got to go home."

"I can do it." Her hands clenched and her eyes narrowed in fierce determination.

I touched her shoulder. "I know you can, but now is not the time for this fight. We need to go home. Up the Haunted Moon Tree." I squeezed her shoulder, my voice low even as the horned and hoofed bandits came ever closer. "Please, we've got to go. Before it's too late. I believe you. I believe in your power. But now is not the time."

Josephine hesitated a moment longer. Then she nodded. My heart soared. I would save her as I had not saved Malachi. In our world, on Earth, we could plan and fortify ourselves. We needed time. We needed safety.

We sprinted through the impossibly tall, purple grass. It was as if we'd stumbled into a purple cornfield. Yet, in front of us stood the Haunted Moon Tree. So huge now, it seemed to rise to the moon above us.

When had it become night?

As before, I leapt for the tree, intending to climb it. Instead, I stumbled and fell flat against the bark of the trunk. It was as if I'd missed a step running down stairs. I stood on the side of the tree, unsteady and confused. Gravity was both beneath and behind me. How?

"Doctor, time is of the essence. We must go." Josephine put a hand to my back and pushed. Then we were running up the tree as if it were on its side. We ran upward, my hair flying behind me. At the same time, we ran forward. Both states of being were possible in this place.

A shot hit the branch in front of me, throwing splinters of wood into my face. I cried out and shielded my eyes. Two more shots. Josephine stumbled.

I turned to her as she got to her feet. Her leg was bleeding. We reached for each other even as the bandits behind-below fired again. This time, it was the spear ballista and it struck true.

Josephine screamed as the spear pierced her through the shoulder. I did not let go. I held both of her hands as she was pushed toward me then pulled backward. "Don't let go."

"I won't," I promised, not knowing I lied despite my sincerity. I saw that the spearhead had a hook to it that prevented it from slipping free from her tortured flesh. I would have to break the spear from behind. "Hold onto me. No matter what happens, hold on."

Josephine nodded, her face grey with pain. "I will. Do what you—"

The rest of her words were lost to the sound of another spear ballista firing. A spearhead punctured Josephine through the chest with an audible breaking of bone and splash of blood. The world froze into flatness and silence. Josephine and I still held both hands in a tight grip. Her mouth opened in the beginnings of a scream that would never come as her body arched with the impact of the spear.

I stared at her, not believing my eyes. Not wanting to believe the death in hers. Unable to make myself move.

Foolishness walked down a branch. He was the only thing moving. "She's dead now. You can let go."

"No. I promised I wouldn't."

"It's fine. I've died many times." The cat cleaned his face with a paw. "At least this was quick for her. She's already dead. She can't feel anything anymore."

"I can't." I stared at Josephine's face frozen in shock and saw that he was correct. There was no life in her eyes. The spear that was still moving toward me had already taken it. "The healing feathers. You must have some. We can save her."

The cat shook his head. "We cannot. The feathers only work on the living."

I watched the spear tip come ever closer to my chest. "I promised her. I can save her body from them. Bring her back from the dead like I did the butterflies?" It was a hopeless question. I already knew the answer.

"You also promised Sati." The cat's tail flicked back and forth, agitated.

I didn't know if I could resurrect Josephine. If I left her, I couldn't for sure. "I can't leave her."

"You can. You must. You have another duty to attend to." The cat reached out a ginger paw to the pocket where the scroll case was. "You can stay here and die with Josephine or you can return to your world to do what needs to be done. Choose."

I thought of Sati's words and wondered if my taking of the Elder Sign is what cost Josephine her life.

Foolishness answered me even though I didn't ask the question aloud. "Her fate was written in the stars long ago. Yours was not. Do you want to die in vain?"

I shook my head and chose to live. Chose to let Josephine fall. With that decision, the world reasserted itself. I jerked back from the spear before it impaled me as well. Josephine was yanked from my hands even as I let her go. I watched her lifeless body plummet into the waiting arms of the minions of the Black Wind. I didn't know what they'd do with her. I didn't want to know.

I turned and ran. Ran for my life, my sanity, my soul, toward the moon. Its fullness filled me. I ran faster. As I reached it, I found myself slumped in my office chair, the single spotlight above and behind Josephine shone in my face.

Across from me with our knees touching, Josephine lay limp in her seat, her eyes closed, her breath non-existent.

Chapter 13

Returning to reality—to Earth, to my office—was both a blessing and a curse. While I knew that I did not know my home at all, I have never been more glad to see familiar surroundings. I thought I was done, free of that place and its frightening truths. I was wrong.

I struggled to a seated position and looked around. The clock on the wall lied to me. No more than fifteen minutes had passed. I couldn't believe it. We'd been in the Dreamlands for hours. I turned from it and reached a hand to Josephine. "Please, God in Heaven, please. Be all right. Be well. Please."

I shook her knee. There was no response. My stomach dropped to the floor. I shook her knee harder before my fingers found her wrist and sought her pulse. It was there. Slow and steady. I wanted to cry. She wasn't dead.

It *had* been a dream after all. I was home. All was going to be well again.

Josephine's eyes fluttered open. She looked around in a panic. She focused in on me, her eyes burning with loss and anger. "I died and you left me." Her voice was soft and intense as she sat up. "I—died."

I moved away, recognizing the high emotion. "It was a dream… our session…the hypnotherapy. It wasn't real. I'm still here."

"Of course it was real." She stood with slow decorum; a woman using every ounce of will not to scream. She covered her face with her hands. "Did you learn nothing during our time in the Dreamlands? It was a *real* dream. A living, real dream, and I died." She pulled her hands down so they only covered her mouth. A gesture of anguish.

Agony tore at my heart. I should have done something, but I hadn't been able to. I reached a hand to her. "It was a dream. It wasn't real. You're here. Alive."

She turned her back to me. "You do *not* understand. You could *never* understand. I can never go back. The stairs are closed to me. I am exiled from my home, my dreaming home."

I moved forward to put a comforting hand on her shoulder. "You will dream. You will still dream."

Josephine whirled, and with a strength born of grief she struck me across the face. I tumbled backward, falling over the low table. Stunned, I lay on the floor, aching from my hard fall. Something within an inner jacket pocket jabbed my breast. As I gathered my senses, Josephine ripped at her dress.

"If it was just a dream, if I am barred from my Dreamlands home, why am I still marked? Why does His mark still burn my breast?"

I saw her upper chest revealed. Upon it were the glowing, writhing, gold marks, beautiful and terrible against her beige skin. If I kept looking, one of those tentacles would move and reveal the eye of the Black Wind…in this world.

My world.

The real world. I refused to see. I turned my face away, ashamed at my cowardice.

"Why can I feel him looking through me? With my way to the Dreamlands barred, why does His mark still burn my soul?" Josephine flung her arms wide in supplication. "Why do I feel this power within, searching for a way out? Why can I do this?"

For a moment, she posed as if martyred. I stood, something metallic falling from my pocket. I thought to chide her for her dramatics—despite the glowing mark upon her breast—but stopped.

The wall nearest her left hand began to warp and melt. I had to remind myself we were no longer in the Dreamlands. Such things did not happen here. "Josephine!" I pointed to the wall. "What's happening?"

My patient turned to the warping wall and tilted her head. It was as if someone had taken a picture of the wall, put it on fabric, and was winding that fabric up from the middle. My bookcase, and all its books, twisted and turned but did not fall from the wall nor the shelf. It was as if they no longer existed in this world. "Josephine, are you doing that?"

Her voice came slow and thoughtful. "Yes. I believe I am. I don't know how. I did not have this power before." Even as she spoke, the glow from her chest intensified. She smiled, wide and mad. "I understand now what happened to me."

I backed away and found myself behind my desk, as far away from the warped reality of my office wall as I could be. With trembling hands, I unlocked the desk and sought my father's gun. I almost collapsed to my knees as I found its cool, solid, metal form. I hadn't lost it in the real world. It was here. What was happening before me was an impossibility. And yet…"What do you understand?" I left the gun in the unlocked drawer—available but not yet at the ready.

"Why I needed to die in the Dreamlands. What my family's pact with the Black Wind is." Josephine reached a hand toward the swirl in reality and tapped it with a single, elegant fingertip. A tiny hole appeared. It did not reveal the office on the other side of the wall. Instead, a faint eldritch light flickered through the small tear in reality.

"Tell me, Josephine. I need to know." I couldn't take my eyes from the hole that looked onto another place and time. The edges of reality shimmered and undulated in a rainbow of colors that reminded me of what I saw as I was pulled into the Dreamlands.

Josephine turned to look at me with three eyes—hers and the Black Wind's. I froze, pinned like prey in bright light. "I have not lost the Dreamlands. I can journey there again at my whim." Pleasure traveled through her words and over her face. "I have not lost my second home."

Behind her, the gate between worlds widened. Through it,

I could see movement. Creatures I recognized—and ones I could not. My mind slid off of these other abominations, refusing to give name to their forms. "You can open a way. You have become one of those meeting points."

"Yes."

"Can you close a gate once you've opened it?"

She blinked at me as if I had said the most absurd thing in the world. "Close the gate? Why would I want to close the gate? This is the power I'm meant to have." A manic joy that bordered on madness danced in her eyes.

I realized I wasn't speaking just to Josephine anymore. I had to reach through the thing influencing her to find her core. I pointed to the hole in reality. "If you can go through, back into the Dreamlands, they can come here. Isn't that so?"

Josephine whirled about and stared through the porthole-sized opening at the oncoming mass of monsters. "That cannot be. They do not belong here. This is my world. They are *not* welcome. I will not have it!" The glow upon her chest diminished in her outrage.

"Then I suggest you close the way." I sounded far calmer than I felt.

She looked down at her chest, at the mark of the Black Wind. When she looked at me again, her eyes cleared from madness to fear. "He is inside me. The Black Wind is doing this."

"Then stop him." I used a tone of command with no expectation of failure.

Josephine furrowed her brow and reached a hand toward the tear. She shook her head. "How? I don't know how. Help me."

"How would you have done it in the Dreamlands?"

"We aren't in the Dreamlands."

I pointed to the widening hole in reality with the minions of the Black Wind running ever closer. "We are. Partly. Use what you know. Use what you've always used. *Fight* him."

Josephine turned back to the window-sized gate and held out her hands. She brought her hands together closer. The gate halted its opening. "It works!" Her triumph was short-lived. The mark upon her breast flared and she fell to her knees with a cry of pain.

I rushed to her side and helped her up. The eye of the Black Wind focused on me, glaring, and I felt my soul quake. I was nothing before its glare. It was hungry and I was food. I would be the first consumed when the Outer God's minions arrived.

"It…He is fighting me." Josephine bowed her head.

"All your life, you've learned to fight, to evade, to escape the Black Wind. Use what you know. I believe in you." As I spoke, the first howls and jeers of the bandits came through the portal. I needed to help as much as I could. If Josephine could at least keep the gate from opening any wider, we would have a good choke point. It would be the Battle of Thermopylae. Hopefully with a better ending.

I squeezed her shoulders. "You know what to do. Fight him. Fight the Black Wind. Close the portal." I stepped back and left her to do what she could while I went for my father's gun. It was not much, but it was something.

A glint of metal from the floor stopped my steps. I had not lost my father's gun to the chasm, but I had returned to this world with another weapon—one I had chosen to carry. A weapon that could help close the gate.

It could also kill Josephine in the process.

I picked up the scroll case. In this reality it was as long as my palm and twice as thick as my thumb. The end cap came off in my hand as if eager to help. The rolled tube of paper was stiff with rough edges. I could still see pieces of the plant fibers that made the paper. It reminded me of papyrus, but every instinct I had screamed that the paper was not of this world.

I unrolled it with careful fingers. Swirling glyphs filled my mind. I don't know how, but I understood what they said. Not the exact words. Only their true intent. I could not grasp it in whole. I understood the concepts. I understood that I could use this spell—for that was what it was—to close and seal this breach between our worlds.

I also understood that it might harm, even kill, Josephine. I looked at her back as she struggled with the tear she'd created. It was smaller, yes, but she would not close it in time. If she died, I didn't know what would happen to the gate. My heart feared for her. The bandits might use their ranged weapons to repeat what had happened in the Dreamlands and murder her in the name of their otherworldly god.

And yet, if I used the spell, it might tear her asunder. It was a choice. A choice only I could make. I couldn't ask her if she would sacrifice herself. Could I? Saving the world from the chaos of the Dreamlands might require a sacrifice. Was there really a choice?

Two things answered my unspoken question at the same time. First, a cyclopean abomination appeared upon the horizon so large I could not find anything to compare it to. It stared at me with its writhing tentacles playing over each other as it moved with impossible speed. Second, Josephine cried out, horror plain in her exhausted voice. "He comes! Doctor, help me!"

I straightened and chose the only path I could. "I have the Elder Sign. I'll use it."

Josephine did not answer. She focused on making the portal smaller, but she only managed to keep it the same size, her body trembling with the effort.

If my patient died, her blood was on my hands.

So be it.

I raised the scroll and began to read in that impossible language. Line by line. After the first sentence, Josephine straightened, a strength flowing into her posture. After the second sentence, she echoed my words. After the third, she echoed my words and drew glowing glyphs, clockwise, in front of the portal, ending with a pentagram to seal it.

"Here on the skin between worlds,
"The dream of pain and exchange awaits.
"Here in the place between death and darkness,
"The threshold spirit lives.

"Tremble at my prayer.
"Tremble as I call.
"Fear this moment in time.
"The threshold spirit denies.

"The way is closed.
"Go.
"The way is denied.
"Go.
"The way is sealed,

"Forever more.
"Go!"

With each line of the spell and Josephine's echoed response, the portal grew smaller. The abominations on the other side of the breach howled their fury. As did the Black Wind. With eldritch might, the Outer God tried to suck Josephine through the portal before it closed, heedless of the damage it would do to her mortal body. A foul wind pulled books and papers from the shelves and my desk. They clattered, fluttered, and thumped to the floor in an unholy cacophony of sound.

I found myself holding Josephine by the waist with one arm and the tatters of the Elder Sign spell in the other hand as we finished closing and sealing the gate together. We yelled the last line, struggling against the grasping wind and the noise that threatened to burst our eardrums.

Then there was nothing.

Chapter 14

When patients have momentous breakthroughs in their therapy, it often looks like a catastrophic breakdown. There can be tears, shouts, curses, temper tantrums, and the tearing of clothing. A psychologist learns to identify a breakthrough in and among patients acting out. After the wild release of emotion, the patient's demeanor tells all. Do they watch to see your reaction or do they turn inward to examine themselves? A breakthrough can be a lovely thing to witness. It can also be destructive and painful. In Josephine's case, her breakthrough saved more than herself.

There was no hole in reality in my office wall. No portal to the Dreamlands. No racing bandits with hooves and horns. No abominations seeking to consume us whole—body and soul.

Josephine and I tumbled to the floor before my unmarred bookcase. My patient sobbed as if her heart were broken. Undoubtedly it was, and would be for a long time to come. Kneeling next to her, I held her tight and rocked her back and forth, grateful she was still alive. I tried to make soothing noises, but my voice was raw from the spell I'd wrought.

Someone shouted at my office door and shook it. The noise of our fight to close the portal had not gone unnoticed. There were at least three voices there, clamoring to get through the locked door. I heard Nurse Heather's strident voice command the rest to move aside.

Still holding and rocking Josephine, I heard the door unlock and watched it flung open. Even as the orderlies rushed in with Hanna and Nurse Heather behind, I threw up a hand, warding them all off. "It's fine. Everything is fine here." I tried to muster as much authority as I could from my kneeling position. My face flushed, my cheek throbbed where Josephine struck me. "We have had…a breakthrough. I believe all will be well now."

Nurse Heather pushed the orderlies aside and gazed at the shambles of my office with a disapproving eye. I could just imagine what she was seeing. I followed her gaze as she visually picked over the books and papers on the floor, the overturned chair—I do not know when that happened—the mess of files and spilled notebooks on my desk. I met her gaze without flinching as she narrowed her eyes at the mark on my cheek.

"This is a new one for you, Dr. Fern. Usually your patients are sappy, sleepy, and pliant. What happened?"

I narrowed my own eyes at the question. "That is between me and my patient."

Nurse Heather put her hands on her hips. "I will need to tell Dr. Mintz something."

"Tell him that Miss Ruggles, my patient, had a breakthrough. We now understand what has been causing her…" I glanced at the girl in my arms and pushed on with the lie, "…hysteria. That is all he needs to know. He will understand."

She gave a thin smile. "I see. I will leave one of the orderlies—"

"You will leave no one. We are fine. In fact, I need all of you…" I met each of their eyes in turn, "…to leave. Now. Nurse Heather, please lock the door again on your way out."

I saw Josephine twitch a hand in a small, peculiar gesture. Even though she still had her face buried in my chest, it was enough. Hanna stepped from the office without a word. Both orderlies glanced between me and Nurse Heather. Silently, they decided they were no longer part of the power struggle. Both retreated to the hallway, taking themselves out of the fight, although they remained close enough to be of use if needed.

I kept my face neutral and bland as Nurse Heather looked over the scene again. I guessed she catalogued all that she saw for her report to Dr. Mintz. I nodded to the door and waited. With that thin smile of disapproval in place, the nurse returned the nod and backed out of the office. She did not take her eyes off me or Josephine until she closed the door between us. I waited until I heard the clack of the lock sliding home before I focused in on Josephine again.

"Can you stand?"

She nodded.

I helped her to her feet. Then left her long enough to set her chair right before guiding her into it. Once seated, she slumped forward, wiping at her face. I settled into my chair. We still sat close, across from one another, our knees almost touching. When Josephine stopped wiping at her face and began to straighten her clothing, I asked, "May we speak about what just happened?"

Josephine cast a furtive glance at her chest before pulling her collar up to her neck. "Yes. I think we must."

"Before all this, you said you understood why he, the Black Wind, wanted you dead in the Dreamlands. What did you realize?"

"That my ancestor was either selfish or stupid." She gazed about the office, frowning at its disarray. "What kind of a man would allow his children and all their children to be marked by an Outer God, to be murdered within the Dreamlands, only to be given the impossible choice of exile from their second home or to bring ruin to this Earth?" She shook her head. "Selfish stupidity. And cruel. The Black Wind cannot take a child as his portal. As children, we are…we are not strong enough to open a gate. It is only with an adult's mind and understanding of what is lost that gives the strength needed to tear a hole between this world and the Dreamlands."

I let out a slow breath, astonished and pleased by her insight. I was not going to have to rip the Dreamlands from my patient another time. She had seen the truth of it immediately. It was as if the child had grown up in the blink of an eye. But now she saw only the loss and not the gain. "Perhaps, but now you have a new duty; a new thing to protect."

She turned bleak eyes to me. A glint of hope shimmered in the distance. "What do you mean?"

"You will need to speak to your mother and demand the information she has on this pact. While you are neither of age nor engaged, you have gone through hell. It is time for you to know what they know. It could be that you are the first in your family history to discover the consequences of the agreement made by your ancestor. You have knowledge. This is power. You must chronicle it for future generations."

Josephine nodded, slow and thoughtful. "Perhaps you are correct." The hope in her eyes transformed into determination.

"There are two other things you must consider." She gave me a quizzical glance. "First, now that this power has manifested within you, there will be those who will wish to use you to open the way between here and the Dreamlands. You must always be on guard."

Josephine smiled a weary smile. "As an heiress, I must also always be on guard. This is nothing new. What is the second thing I must consider?"

"Your beloved friend, Mimi, is Professor Sati Das. She is a patient here. You are not alone."

Her eyes widened in surprise and joy. "She is? She's here?"

"Didn't you wonder how I knew her in the Dreamlands?"

Josephine waved a dismissive hand. "Dream logic. Such things happen all the time. There was no need to question it." She leaned forward, eager. "I want to see her."

"I shall try. I think she will be pleased to see you in this reality." I half-frowned. "Assuming we can get her out of the clutches of Dr. Mintz. That might be difficult. She is a visiting professor who has no family here as far as I can tell."

Josephine sat up straight, raising her chin. "That is where money comes into play. I will have my lawyers get her out of the asylum and bring her to my home." She paused and considered this for a moment, tapping a finger to her lip before folding her hands together once more. "I will need to find out which university sponsored her to study here and on what project. The invitation to host their visiting professor should spur things in motion. No matter. My lawyers will make my wishes known in the appropriately persuasive manner."

I breathed a soft sigh of relief. Josephine would be fine. She no longer looked to me for all the answers. I touched her knee with a gentle hand. "You realize you cannot talk about this with anyone except me and your most trusted people. Only to those who know the reality of your family." From the blank politeness in her eyes, she did not understand what I was trying to say. I opted for bluntness. "You must admit to being hysterical. That you had a bad period, but we found the source of your fear." The stubbornness set in on her face as she thought this over. It cleared when she realized I was correct

"Which is what?" Her voice, both resigned and wary.

I considered for a moment. "How long have your parents been on tour?"

"About two months."

"Have they been on tour since your brother died?"

Josephine shook her head. The light of realization came into her expression. "I feared for the loss of my parents? When Leland left, he died?"

I nodded. "It was a bout of hysteria brought on by the memory of your brother." I touched her knee again. "We will need to continue our sessions. Though, they will be at your home. There is still much you will need to work through."

That determination dimmed. She nodded. "I am exhausted."

"I would like to keep you here for another week. Daily sessions. Then you will go home. It will give your servants enough time to prepare. If I can get you in to see Professor Das, I will. If not…"

"I will allow my lawyers to deal with Dr. Mintz."

"Yes. In the meantime, you will have much to consider. I would like to have you off all medication for this week. I want to make certain there are no lingering aftereffects of our journey into the Dreamlands and the removal of the book. I will give your maid sleeping pills to hold. If it appears you still need them or prefer not to dream…"

Her lips tightened into a line of remembered pain before she nodded. "Thank you, Doctor…Carolyn. I will try to be strong—for all of us."

It was all I could ask her to do. In return, I needed to be strong for me and my sanity. I wondered what I would dream of this night. Or, if I could, would I return to the Dreamlands on my own? Even now, the remembered whispers of the eldritch book I had held still called to me.

Epilogue

*D*ear Future Carolyn,
I do not know whether you will believe everything I have had to say when you read this in the coming years and consider your past, but I feel I must write what I remember of my time in the Dreamlands and of my patient, Josephine Ruggles.

Three days have passed since the hypnotherapy session with Josephine that changed our lives forever. Josephine's bleeding nightmares are gone, but the reality of her loss is still settling in. There is no question of trust between us. We journeyed through hell together and came out with a bond that can never be broken—whether or not I want it to be. She trusts me. She relies on me. She talks to me. She is so much better. I feel I honor Malachi's memory with every successful turn she makes.

My duty as her doctor is to be there to a point. That line has blurred with our shared experience. I must tread carefully in our sessions. There will come a point where we discuss the fact that I was unable to save her from the bandits in the Dreamlands—that I chose to leave her body behind—and that resulted in the loss of access to her beloved "dreaming home." Then I will find out if she blames me in any way. I am an easy target and she still has so much rage and grief within her.

In truth, much of what happened in the Dreamlands has faded from my mind. I find myself referring back to previous notes with wonder and some skepticism—despite the fact that I lived these memories. I know it all happened, but as with dreams, only specific details remain. All else fades, leaving an incoherent string of thoughts and images.

Still, I continue to write down everything I can remember. Every detail of every creature encountered: the zoog, the cats of Ulthar, the shantak, the feathers from the little red bird of Celephaïs, the goat-legged bandits with hooves and horns, the guardians at the gates between the Seventy Steps of Light Slumber and the Seven Hundred Steps of Deeper Slumber, and the Dreamlands themselves.

I admit my fear to writing down anything about the Black Wind. I fear bringing the god's attention to me again after I thwarted the plan to use Josephine as a gateway between our worlds. That hunger I felt will haunt my dreams—waking and sleeping—forevermore. It is why the fading of details does not upset me as much as it could. I know when I look back on these notes and read them with a more experienced and jaded eye, I will read them without the immediacy of memory or fear.

Tell me, future Carolyn, does the nameless dread I feel now in the pit of my soul ever go away? How many more times do we fight the Outer Gods? Or the Elder Gods? What do we lose each time we do?

I am being dramatic. I will move on before the fear grows again.

In other news, Dr. Mintz is less than pleased at Miskatonic University's renewed attention to Professor Sati Das. It seems that the university is more than pleased to have piqued the interest of a well-to-do young woman such as Miss Josephine Ruggles and, of course, the Ruggles pocketbook.

Once Sati is ensconced within the Ruggles household, I will be able to speak to her in depth about the Dreamlands. I can only hope she will able to answer some of my lingering questions. I have some concerns as to her mental well-being now that she carries the awakened book that drove Josephine mad.

Until then, I will care for Josephine as best I can. The next couple of weeks will bring interesting changes. I look forward to them.

This afternoon, I will walk through Arkham with renewed eyes.

I wonder which details, that once held no meaning, will come to light and change my perspective of my home? Sati is right. The scales have fallen from my eyes and I am changed forever. I find myself both eager and afraid to discover what I will see with my newborn sight.

Until next time,
Present day Caroline

About the Author

Jennifer Brozek is a Hugo Award–nominated editor and a Bram Stoker–nominated author. Winner of the Australian Shadows Award for best-edited publication, Jennifer has edited fifteen anthologies with more on the way, including the acclaimed *Chicks Dig Gaming* and *Shattered Shields* anthologies. Author of *Apocalypse Girl Dreaming*, *Industry Talk*, the *Karen Wilson Chronicles*, and the acclaimed *Melissa Allen* series, she has more than seventy published short stories and is the Creative Director of Apocalypse Ink Productions.

Jennifer is a freelance author for numerous RPG companies. Winner of the Scribe, Origins, and ENnie awards, her contributions to RPG sourcebooks include *Dragonlance*, *Colonial Gothic*, *Shadowrun*, *Serenity*, *Savage Worlds*, and *White Wolf SAS*. Jennifer is the author of the award-winning YA Battletech novel *The Nellus Academy Incident* and Shadowrun novella *Doc Wagon 19*. She has also written for the AAA MMO *Aion* and the award-winning videogame *Shadowrun Returns*.

When she is not writing her heart out, she is gallivanting around the Pacific Northwest in its wonderfully mercurial weather. Jennifer is an active member of SFWA, HWA, and IAMTW. Read more about her at www.jenniferbrozek.com or follow her on Twitter at @JenniferBrozek.

HISTORIC FIND IN ESSEX FALLS?

Reconstructed fragments of the original shards found at Eltdown on display.

Mr. Gideon Sarvis, a hiker enjoying a trek through Essex Falls, came across a small pile of pottery shards recently unearthed during an earthquake. An amateur archaeologist, he noted that the pottery shards were not known to the region; they had been made with a pre-historic clay not found in the Essex Falls area and adorned with ancient symbols he had never seen before. Marking the spot on his map, he collected several samples and sent them to the Miskatonic University for study.

The Essex Falls shards caused quite the uproar amongst the history professors at the university because they appear to be nearly identical to the Eltdown Shards, which contain symbols that challenge everything scientists currently know about Earth's history.

The original Eltdown Shards are pottery fragments of unknown origin found in Eltdown in southern England in 1882. The shards have been dated back to the Triassic Period—the first period of Mesozoic Era—which occurred between 251 million and 199 million years ago. The pottery fragments are covered in symbols that have not yet been translated. The Eltdown Shards continue to be a source of contention amongst scientists, historians, and archaeologists, as the earliest known human petroglyphs date back only twelve thousand years.

After much debate within the halls of Miskatonic University, Professor Sati Das of St. Hilda's College at Oxford University, an expert on the Eltdown Shards, was invited to perform her own examination of the pottery shards found at Essex Falls. Professor Das has accepted the invitation and will arrive within the month.

Should the Essex Falls pottery shards match the shards found at Eltdown, it will reignite the continued argument on whether the shards are a hoax that now crosses continents or are instead the archaeological find of the millennium.

I had another nightmare last night. I suppose I must face my terror and examine what I know of the horned and hoofed minions of the Black Wind. If I do not, I fear I will never stop dreaming of them.

First, Sati assures me they are not demons, merely goat-legged creatures—I will not call them men—with horns. I do not recall seeing goat ears within their wild hair. That may be a flaw in my observation.

Physically, these creatures appeared to be akin to the classical satyr. They stood as tall as an average man, perhaps a bit shorter. Their goat legs were no uniform color, although their hooves appeared to be black. They wore torn pants and kilts. No shoes (obviously). Almost all of them were shirtless or wore only a vest or sash, revealing muscular torsos and chests. Upper body hair was inconsistent. The horns were relatively uniform: large, protruding from the forehead, and curved backward.

As for their faces, I do not remember. In my mind's eye, some of them did not have faces at all—just a blur where their faces should have been. Others had the kind of face one would expect from a bandit: rough, unshaven, dirty, with broken teeth. Usually open in a leer or a shout.

My memory of these creatures appearance is doubly flawed. First, how much of their appearance was influenced by my own experiences and prejudices? I consciously manipulated things in the Dreamland. Did I unconsciously manipulate what I saw of our pursuers? That would account for the blurred faces. They were too horrible to contemplate or to translate.

Second, how much of this is what I saw, and how much of this is detail I am filling in as my memory fades? The mind will make up details to make certain things make sense. We look for patterns. We fill in details to suit the patterns we have detected.

Something to consider going forward.

Also of note: Sati says that these creatures are usually more pirate than bandit, preferring to attack their prey on the oceans and wide rivers of the Dreamlands rather than pursuing their quarry on land. This explains the incongruous nature of their dress—or lack thereof: it is better suited to a boat rather than the land. This also accounts for their intimidating vocalization designed to terrify and stun their victims. I imagine it would be very effective on the water, where there is no place to flee. Most importantly, this explains their expert use of the ballista spear weapon. It is not the kind of weapon easily transported on land. Aboard a pirating vessel, however, it would be right at home and quite effective at piercing and pulling in other ships, and then keeping them close enough to board.

The more I grasp for details about the minions of the Black Wind, the more my mind refuses to relay them. It is as though part of me wants to forget they exist. I pray I have written enough to banish these abominations from my nightmares.

I know there is no danger of them in my normal dreams. That does not stop me from waking with the feeling of an unsettled dread that leaves my stomach queasy and my heart thumping for most of the morning. I flinch at shadows and small reflective surfaces. I somehow expect to see them pursuing in the distance. Unexpected sounds on the street have me seeking cover before I realize what I am doing. In the back of my mind, I am always watching, listening, waiting for sign of their pursuit—as if they are not yet done with me.

This persistent fear is something I must fight. I am to be the rock for my patients. I cannot come into a session myself lost at sea. Truth be told, however, focusing on my work soothes my unquiet mind. There is a lesson in that. I think I will work to find it.

It finally happened. I dreamed of the Dreamlands. I believe it was a normal dream on the cusp of becoming a dream within the Dreamlands. I have a chance to return. It will take some effort, but I am very excited to know I have at least a chance. I wonder how many other people have the opportunity to visit another world—and never realize it.

Last night, I decided to see whether I could enter the Dreamlands and consciously set my mind to make the effort. I told myself as I went to bed that I would enter the Dreamlands. I focused all my thoughts on the Seventy Steps of Light Slumber. Everything I could remember of them—the sound of my steps upon the stairs, my hesitant gait, the feeling of fear and anticipation of being someplace so unexpected and unreal, and yet so very real. I remembered how far away Josephine and the Guardians had seemed from the top of the stairs and how the gates disappeared into the sky above. There was a particular feeling of crossing from one room to another. Or from the outside into a once-familiar house.

I know I was thinking of the steps as I fell asleep. Thus, I was not surprised when I found myself in the same stone corridor Josephine had pulled me into on her way to the Seventy Steps of Light Slumber. When I recognized it, I tested my hypothesis and changed my clothing into something better suited to adventures. When it worked, I let the dream take me.

I am glad I have experience in lucid dreaming. It has come in handy more times that I had ever expected.

Outside the corridor of stone, a path of concrete led to the edge of a familiar cliff. There was no childlike Dr. Mintz to warn me off. I knew what I was doing and where I wanted to go. This time, the stairs were like the marble steps in the Orne Library, and the handrail had the same wooden feel. Much like walking a path in the woods over and over, familiarity brings comfort and allows for greater observation. The stairs were not as steep or as frightening as the first time. The wind was light and fresh. The chasm below was obscured by fluffy clouds, as was the sky above. Things flew within those clouds, too far away for me to identify. Yet, I knew I had nothing to fear because I knew where I was going. My comfort brought with me a comforting environment.

Nevertheless, I counted each step. Seventy in all. My heart pounded with excitement and my breath caught in my throat.

At the bottom, I faced the Guardians, Nasht and Kaman-Tha, who stood in my way once more. They were not as tall as before, but they were still hooded and robed, hiding their bearded faces from me. Neither held a weapon.

I said, "I would pass into the Dreamlands."

Nasht, the black robed one, shook his head. "No. You are not prepared this time."

"I am," I protested. "I have changed my clothing. I know how to control my dreams."

"You are not strong enough," came Kaman-Tha's reply. "It is easy to be strong for another. Less so to be strong for only yourself."

"What do you mean?" I asked.

"You were protecting Josephine. The whole of your being was about her. If you go now, you will be lost." They were both speaking in my head. "You need to find your core self before you can go farther."

"But I have changed my clothing. I can do this."

"No. If you could, the Gate to the Seven Hundred Steps of Deeper Slumber would already be open." They both waved a dismissive hand at me and I fell backward.

I jerked awake in my bed. When I spoke to Josephine and Sati about this, they conferred and then told me they would devise a plan of study to strengthen my mind to allow me into the Dreamlands. I am both excited and terrified at this prospect.

I do not know why I want to return. I simply know that I do. Perhaps that is also part of my problem. Perhaps I need a focus, a purpose to go there. I will need to think on this more.

The Zoog appear to be marsupial, intelligent, and group oriented. In the short time I was able to watch them, they worked together, feinting and flanking their prey. I suspect they use cooperative hunting tactics, much like the Harris's Hawk. In this case, it was to distract the greater foe in Josephine while using stealth in an attempt to capture the intended prey of Foolishness. My intervention distracted them, causing them to abandon their assault.

Once they saw me and recognized my superior weaponry—my father's pistol, its ability to do damage, and my skill—they immediately attempted to recruit me to their side. Not necessarily to have me attack the cat, but to have me become their ally in general. I suspect this is because I did not attack them. Instead, I warned them. The Zoog appeared to be focused on the immediate and immediate results without considering anything else about me. They did not know whether I could be a good ally or not. They saw me use the pistol, and that determined their choice.

On the other hand, the Cats of Ulthar appear to be individualistic, intelligent mammals with a singular higher power to which they pay homage. As the "eyes and ears of Ulthar," each cat appears to have an individual duty of a sort. For Foolishness, it is to act foolishly. For Insightful, it is to bring insight to those who have need of it—

whether they know it or not. For Comfort, it is to bring emotional and mental comfort for those who are suffering. Even now, just thinking of that beautiful black cat, I can feel the warmth and comfort of her presence. It is as if she were sitting in my lap once more.

The Cats of Ulthar appear to be focused more on the future rather than the present. Everything they do seems to be linked to what is to come. There is a hierarchy. That much was obvious through my interactions with Insightful and the way she commanded both the humans and the cats around her. The same goes for the cats who watched Foolishness lead us about town but did not approach.

In essence, it seems that the Cats of Ulthar are almost the exact opposites of the Zoog. This brings me to another point. The antagonistic relationship between the Zoog and the Cats of Ulthar appears to be an unpleasant necessity rather than a true enmity. Something that helps keep the status quo of the Dreamlands.

It makes sense that to repeat something as "foolish" as walking alone within the Enchanted Wood—knowing full well that the Zoog will attack—sets up a pattern that keeps the Dreamlands around the event stable and keeps the Haunted Moon Tree in the same place within the Enchanted Wood. When a strong enough will can change the fabric of reality, stability is to be prized and sought after above all—no matter how "foolish" or painful it appears.

I wonder whether all of the denizens and creatures of the Dreamlands have the same duty. Do the hoofed and horned minions of the Black Wind always pursue and harry their quarry at the order of the Black Wind? Do the shantak always attack anyone who comes up the mountain path on their way to reach the valley where the Red House resides? Is the Red House always a safe haven, while attacks always come at the transitions? Do patterns of repeated behavior set the rules to a world like the Dreamlands?

There is so much to consider: so many questions and so little in the way of concrete answers. I suppose Josephine would say something like, "Such is the way of the Dreamlands." It is easy for her to take everything for granted. She has learned the rules of the Dreamlands in that automatic way that children learn appropriate manners without knowing why they are appropriate.

Although I did not see the miraculous "little red singing bird of Celephaïs," I did feel its healing effects. I spoke to Josephine about this incredible creature. She told me that it was about the size of a large wren and lived all over the Dreamlands, regardless of the climate. It was as comfortable in caves as it was the tundra of the north, the forests of the west, and the jungles to the south.

When I asked her why it was "of Celephaïs," she explained that the story of the bird had come to her through her parents. There is a wondrous city called Celephaïs "in the Valley of Ooth-Nargai beyond the Tanarian Hills." In that place, demigods had come to trade with other people of the Dreamlands and of Earth. The little red birds with healing properties first came from there, and then the birds made the rest of the Dreamlands their home. To honor their origins, everyone remembers that the little red singing birds are "of Celephaïs."

I asked her where this marvelous city was, but all she could tell me was "across the Cerenerian Sea, where the ocean meets the sky." When I pressed her for more details—where Ooth-Nargai and the Tanarian Hills were—she asked me where Australia was and where within it was Perth. I stopped my questions when I realized I could not accurately answer her without consulting a globe. At least now I know the name of the large body of water within the Dreamlands and the names of other places. Details like these are what press me to question Josephine all the more. She does not realize all that she knows.

Back to the little red bird. Its healing abilities appear to be two-fold. The first—and more powerful—healing ability was its song. Merely listening to the bird's song soothed the unsettled mind. It is akin to the power that Comfort, the cat of Ulthar, used to soothe me by her very presence. I liken it to a psychic sedative. The relaxing of a muscle often makes a wound hurt less. When I was faced with the realization that I was no longer on Earth—that what I was experiencing was, in fact, real—I wanted to reject the idea as "impossible." Relaxing my mind and letting go of what I knew was what I needed to allow myself to be receptive to a new paradigm.

I have so many questions about this little bird and its healing song. The first of which is why can I not remember it? If I could remember the song, would it continue to heal my mind? Could we record the melody and use it to heal the minds of some of the most unfortunates within the asylum? Probably not, although it bears further study.

The second healing ability of this remarkable bird was its feathers. Each feather was small, about the length of my thumb and as wide at its widest point. These feathers were placed into and across my wounds. They stung at first, and then melted into my flesh, healing it as they disappeared. The feathers seemed to become a part of my body, replacing and repairing the wounded area as if they had always been part of it. The feathers left no scars. It was as though the wound had never happened.

Would they work outside the Dreamlands? Or is that ability only allowed there because, within the Dreamlands, the feathers of the little red singing bird of Celephaïs heal?

Testing this is one of the reasons I wish to return to the Dreamlands—whether or not the Guardians at the Gate between the Seventy Steps of Light Slumber and the Seven Hundred Steps of Deeper Slumber agree. Eventually, I will return.

It would be so much easier if I had Josephine by my side. I still do not quite understand why her death within the Dreamlands bars her from ever returning in dreams. Dying in dreams does not kill you in mortal life. I suppose it is just another one of the rules of the Dreamlands I will continue to not understand.

Perhaps I can meet up with Sati and she can escort me in. I will ask the next time we meet.

As expected, Josephine remained within the asylum for only another four days. I told her we would need a week to see whether she was truly healed or whether she would rebel against me. She informed me on the third day without nightmares or drugs that she would be going home the next day and that she had already send word to her household to come get her. It was a fait accompli. She felt it was only polite to tell me.

She also wanted to let me know what her lawyers had discovered about Professor Sati Das and that they had already made a two-pronged advance on getting the professor out of the asylum and into the Ruggles household. It certainly pays to have the kind of capital that young woman has at her disposal.

Miskatonic University had been informed of Miss Ruggles's interest in the professor's project involving the study of the Essex Shards—that is something to examine later—and the asylum had been informed that the professor would be leaving posthaste at the university's request. I am certain there was some sort of financial impetus to convince the university to get their visiting professor out of the asylum as soon as possible.

It was a full week before I was able to see Josephine in the sanctuary of her home. Too many other patients needed my attention. Interesting that Dr. Mintz suddenly finds my opinion "invaluable." I suspect the lawyers included words like "grateful" and "donation to the Arkham Sanatorium" as they informed Dr. Mintz he was losing a patient because of my "cured" patient. There will always be more patients for him to experiment on.

Speaking of patients, Josephine is still very much my patient. Her parents were on the other side of the world when word reached them of their daughter's breakdown. I believe it will still be another couple of weeks until they return from their tour, and they may not skip the rest of their tour now that Josephine is out of the asylum and at home, recovering from her "hysterical episode."

The reality of her situation rests heavy upon her shoulders and mind. Not only has she lost the ability to go to a place dear to her heart, she has gained the power to possibly destroy our world. She is going through the grieving process. She admits to her fury at me and at Professor Das, but she understands I am a convenient target, and the professor's culpability is debatable.

Despite her extreme emotions, Josephine still looks to me for guidance and help. I am doing the best I can. We are treating this like the loss of a limb, complete with phantom pain. She is still marked by the Black Wind and she will need to fight him for the rest of her life—as well as to teach her children to fight him like she has.

Fortunately, she will not need to do it alone. Beyond Sati and myself, there are others. One of her dreaming friends, Luke Robinson, sent Josephine a letter recently. It arrived the afternoon of our session. I do not know what he said, but it seemed to cheer her up immensely.

I have begun to recognize the signs of others knowing the truth of our world and the hidden doors into different places and times. There are glyphs about town. I have begun to bring these back to both Josephine and Sati to see whether they know what the symbols mean. Sometimes they know; other times they do not. Sometimes they know but keep their own counsel. It can be frustrating.

I am straddling a dangerous and complicated line with Josephine. She is my patient. Now, she is also my friend. In some respects, she is also my mentor. We are still working out the boundaries for when we are in each role: doctor/patient, friends, mentor/mentee.

Josephine is a young woman of incredible will and stubbornness. She was born into the role she plays and is not used to being questioned or challenged outside of certain situations. I admire her as much as she frustrates me. I must frustrate her as well. It will take time and experience for the two of us to pin down who we are with each other when we are within our respective circumstances.

Despite the confusion, fear, and occasional nightmares I still suffer, I am glad we met and I was able to help her. Josephine is a good woman. I am better for knowing her. This world around me is not what I thought it once was. It will be Josephine, and those like her, who help me understand what I must learn now.

In the end, Josephine was the one to give me a new goal: to stop the "Darkness that Watches." It or its forces killed my patient, Malachi, and it is a danger to any other unfortunates who cross it. No more patients should have to die like Malachi did. Not if I have the opportunity to stop the madness before it begins.

I just had my second meeting with Professor Sati Das in the flesh. For the most part, she is doing well, although I can see the strain of the book on the Eltdown Shards in her eyes and in her distraction. She pretends she is fine, but the signs of trauma are there. I can only imagine what she is going to through. She will not tell me how she has tamed the book. I think whatever she has done is a temporary measure. I want to help more than I have, more than I can.

In some ways, I believe we are each other's patients. She needs help understanding what happened to her and how to cope with the guilt of what her actions with Josephine ultimately led to. I need help understanding more about the Dreamlands and the other worlds that surround this one. That, and the terror of the Outer Gods.

Sati is a woman experienced with both the knowledge and horror of these otherworldly beings of power that want to consume our world. She is also familiar with magic. Real, mind-breaking, reality-altering magic. She still does not know what sent her into a coma and then plunged her into madness. She believes it has something to do with her study of the Eltdown Shards. She believes it is possible that magic was involved, but her memory of the incident is gone. Repressed. She has asked me to use my hypnotic technique to help her recover those memories. I have agreed to do so.

We both realize that I need to know about the true nature of the universe in order to help her. Unfortunately, this is where Sati's academic training clashes with my medical training. She cannot figure out where to begin to tell me what I need to know about the archaeological work she does or how it links into the other worlds we have encountered.

I would like her to begin at the beginning. It is the only sensible thing to do. It will give me a foundation to build my questions on and allow me to guide her through the hypnotic session with greater accuracy.

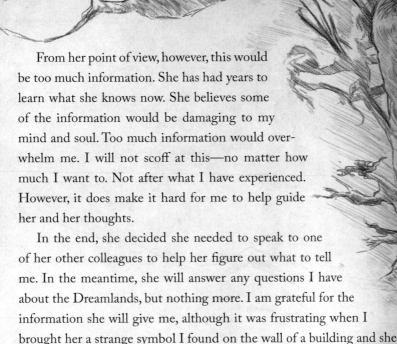

From her point of view, however, this would be too much information. She has had years to learn what she knows now. She believes some of the information would be damaging to my mind and soul. Too much information would over-whelm me. I will not scoff at this—no matter how much I want to. Not after what I have experienced. However, it does make it hard for me to help guide her and her thoughts.

In the end, she decided she needed to speak to one of her other colleagues to help her figure out what to tell me. In the meantime, she will answer any questions I have about the Dreamlands, but nothing more. I am grateful for the information she will give me, although it was frustrating when I brought her a strange symbol I found on the wall of a building and she refused to tell me anything, even though she clearly recognized it.

"You are not ready" and "It is too dangerous for you just now" are the two refrains I hear most. I am tired of them. Sati and Josephine are of like mind on this. I cannot budge either of them. This protectiveness is mad-dening. I cannot force either of them to give me the information I seek.

However, if they continue to insist on moving too slowly, I shall need to find someone who will tell me something. Obviously, there is more to this than the Dreamlands. There is, at the very least, a place called R'lyeh and another called the Plateau of Leng. I feel like I am at the top of an iceberg with most of the information I need below the surface of the water.

Perhaps I should visit that Professor Walters that Sati seems to know so well. Perhaps he is more than the aging academic he appears to be and will tell me what I need to know.

COME OUT TO THE RINK IN
INDEPENDENCE SQUARE

PUBLIC SKATING

The F

YOUR

TEN PAGES

ARKHA

MISKATONIC UNIVERSITY RARE BOOK ROOM DEDICATION CEREMONY

Arkham, M.A., Jan. 12—Yesterday, the Ruggles Rare Book Room in the Miskatonic University Library was formally dedicated to Thomas Ruggles by his son and daughter-in-law, Alonzo and Nina Ruggles, respectively. More than seventy people—including librarians, city administrators, deans, and Ruggles family members and friends—attended the ceremony. The Ruggles Rare Book Room is named in honor of the Ruggles family, who are longtime patrons of Miskatonic University, the Orne Library, and many of the academic research and restoration projects hosted by the Orne Library.

Pascal Ruggles was the first of the Ruggles family to support Miskatonic University back in 1835, when he donated several of the Orne Library's prized possessions including *The Wonders of the Invisible World* by Cotton Mather, written in 1692; the *Malleus Maleficarum* ("The Hammer of Witches") by Henricus Institoris, written in 1486; and *The Invisible Worlds Adjacent to Ours* by Wistan Eckels, written in 1702. All three of these important novels now have a permanent home in the Ruggles Rare Book Room.

As part of the university celebrations, the Ruggles Rare Book Room dedication began with the Naming of the Patrons as well as a schedule of forthcoming improvements to the university. This specific thanking of past and present patrons has become a time-honored tradition, and it is designed to remind one and all of the historical importance of patronage as well as of those who have given so much to make Miskatonic University the august establishment it is today.

There was a ribbon-cutting ceremony followed by a candlelit observance led by Alonzo Ruggles and Librarian Abigail Foreman dedicating the new room to Thomas Ruggles. Each attendee was asked to hold a candle and circle the new room while Alonzo and Ruth recited a poem in ancient Sumerian—a favorite of Thomas Ruggles. It was a solemn ceremony befitting the serious nature of the new library room. The candles were a particularly fortunate occurrence, as the electric lights failed part way through the recitation.

The Ruggles Rare Book Room was designed by obscure architect Roger Mortimer, an adherent to modern architectural theory. While the architectural form of the room is simplicity itself, the ornamental details are what make the room the spectacular piece of art that it is. Instead of working in heavy, sober woods and colors, Mortimer's design focused on the interplay between light and dark, acute and obtuse angled lines, and the intricate weaving of different types of wood. The floor of the Ruggles Rare Book Room highlights this with its swirling design built from alternating colored, oddly shaped pieces of wood laid out in a labyrinthine pattern. The pattern gave more than one attendee a sense of vertigo after staring at the motif for too long. This design breathes life into a room normally used for somber, solitary research by some of the world's foremost literary scholars.

Mr. Mortimer was unable to attend the dedication ceremony.

When interviewed, Head Librarian Dr. Henry Armitage explained the

CONTINUED ON PAGE 2

MISKATONIC PLAYHOUSE PRESENTS

RARE BOOK ROOM DEDICATION (CON'T)

importance of the new room to the Orne Library. "Finally, the special collections—our rare books, the Arkham Collection, and the university archives—have, at last, obtained an appropriate and protected room to be stored and displayed within. They need special care and attention. Now they have it. We thank the Ruggles family, and Thomas Ruggles in particular, for their keen insight on the importance of these rare books."

Thomas Ruggles was born June 13, 1846, in New York City. He moved to Arkham to become a journalist and a novelist. He put himself through college as a reporter and a handyman for the *Arkham Gazette*, gaining a reputation as a polite but quirky student. Although he came from a well-to-do family, Ruggles was known to follow his dreams first—both figuratively and literally. He dreamed of making it on his own without the assistance of his family, and he was determined to make that dream come true. Once he did—working his way up the ranks of the *Arkham Gazette* to Senior Editor before moving back to New York—he felt he could accept his family's money. Finally, he began Ruggles Publishing and became one of the premiere publishers in the United States.

Married to Agatha Kent, Ruggles never wanted for a social life. Ever in demand, he and his wife frequented the most desirable places in New York, enjoying the company of his peers and foreign scholars less suited to such well-to-do establishments. Despite being an iconoclastic rebel, Ruggles was a man of faith as well as scholarship. He led an active life within the Holy Stone Parish, where he was known for quoting obscure literature and using heretical parables as historical touchstones for teaching lessons.

In 1906, Ruggles retired from running Ruggles Publishing, handing the rein over to his competent and knowledg

able son, Alonzo Ruggles. At that time, he returned to Arkham, stating that he had dreamed that his old life was done and he needed to return to where he belonged. Ruggles spent his days around his beloved university library books when he was not traveling. He would tell one of his near constant companions, "My dreams call. I must go." Then he would be off on tour.

An experienced and active traveler, Ruggles visited England, Germany, Austria, Switzerland, and France, as well as the African continent, often bringing back obscure tomes of esoteric knowledge that he would later donate to the Orne Library. He ceased his travel when the Great War erupted. After that, he focused on ways to, as the dedication plaque states, "guide the novice, transmit culture, and provide information in times of chaos."

While the Miskatonic University Library is open to the public on a limited basis, the Ruggles Rare Book Room is reserved for university students, alumni, and partners.